What Lies Behind You

What Lies Behind You

Robert Furlani

Writers Club Press
San Jose New York Lincoln Shanghai

What Lies Behind You

Writers Club Press
an imprint of iUniverse.com, Inc.

For information address:
iUniverse.com, Inc.
5220 S 16th, Ste. 200
Lincoln, NE 68512
www.iuniverse.com

ISBN: 0-595-20310-8

Printed in the United States of America

For my mother and father, Edward and Helen, with gratitude for all they have taught me in life. For my wife, Anne Marie, for her unending patience and support, and for my children, Jenna, Rob and Joshua, for their love.

What lies behind you and what lies before you are tiny matters compared to what lies within you.

Ralph Waldo Emerson

CHAPTER I

1983

Robert Paolucci sat on the green glider in the corner of the backyard and began to open the strongbox he had unearthed a moment earlier. A shovel and pickaxe lay at his feet. His face was swollen and bruised, his clothes, bloody and torn. A throbbing pain pounded in his head.

His father had buried the metal box under a large white rock in the corner garden on the morning of the day he died, more than twenty years ago. The box and its contents had been carefully wrapped in plastic. He had known that two decades would pass before he would have the opportunity to tell his son where to look.

The hinges creaked and moaned as Robert carefully pried the rusted lid with a screwdriver. Inside he found a satchel containing his father's laboratory notes and two manilla envelopes; one was addressed to him, the other to his 1mother. He tore open his envelope and found a handwritten letter, his great grandfather's pocket watch and a St. Christopher's pendant attached to a silver chain. Robert examined the pendant for a moment, turned it over and read the inscription:

What lies behind you and what lies before you are tiny matters when compared with what lies within you.

He held the pendant in the palm of his hand, slowly closed his fingers around it, and squeezed tightly. He sat back, closed his eyes and took a deep breath, trying in vain to clear the rush of emotions that choked his thoughts. He hadn't slept more than ten hours in the past three days and, until this moment, hadn't realized just how tired and sore his body felt.

"Hey, are you all right? I've called you three times already," Helen Paolucci yelled, interrupting her son's momentary solitude.

He slowly turned toward the direction of her voice and nodded feebly. He looked tired and weak. She was a few yards away when she noticed the pile of dirt, the hole in the garden where the white rock had laid, and the lockbox sitting alongside her son on the glider. It took a few more steps for her to discover the bruises on his face, and dried blood on his jacket.

"Oh my god, what happened to you?" she cried, rushing to his side.

"I'm okay, Mom. Really, I am. Let's go inside, there's something I need to tell you. It's about Dad."

He took his mother by the hand and led her to the house. As they reached the back door, he looked over his shoulder and noticed that the glider was bathed in bright sunlight that had somehow squeezed its way through the dense leaves of his father's maple trees. A sad smile came to his face as he followed the sunlight through the towering trees to the falling sun.

"Goodbye, Dad, I love you with all my heart," he whispered. A tear rolled off his cheek and an overwhelming feeling of emptiness settled in the pit of his stomach.

A moment later, a solitary storm cloud drifted across the amber sky, chasing the sunlight away just as the screen door closed behind him.

CHAPTER 2

1960

Seven-year-old Robert Paolucci bounded down the porch steps with a paper bag in his hand. "Hey, Dad, wait! You forgot your lunch," he yelled, leaping off the second to last step and rushing to his father's car.

Edward rolled down the window, grabbed the brown paper bag and kissed his son goodbye. "Thanks kiddo. I'll see you tonight."

"Can we play a game of catch when you get home? I want to break in my new Mickey Mantle mitt."

"Sure can. We'll go to the park after dinner," Edward said as he backed the car out of the driveway and started down the street.

As soon as his car turned the corner, a black convertible slipped away from the curb and followed, staying just out of sight. The driver flicked a spent cigarette onto the street and quickly rolled up the heavily tinted window. But, not before Robert caught a glimpse of his imposing silhouette.

       *   *   *

"He's in there waiting for you," Norma Maxwell said as Edward poked his head in the office door. He was running twenty minutes late for his weekly meeting with his boss, Michael Anderson.

"What time did he get in?"

"I walked in at seven-thirty and he was already working on his second pot of coffee. He looks terrible. Like he spent the night here again and he's in one foul mood. Major Adams has already called twice this morning. What a way to end the week, huh?"

"Thanks for the warning. How are you holding up?"

"I'll be fine. I'm out of here at five and off to Cleveland for John's graduation."

"That's great. I still can't believe your son's graduating from college already."

"They sure grow up fast. Yours will be graduating before you know it. I remember when Johnny was his age and it doesn't seem all that long ago."

Edward smiled. "Well here I go. Wish me luck."

"Better you than me," Norma grinned.

He walked into the large office and tossed his coat on the brown leather sofa next to the door. Michael's face was buried in the pile of papers that covered his desk. Four large matching wood file cabinets stood adjacent to his oak desk. Files were scattered everywhere. Some rested on the tops of open file cabinet drawers, others were stacked in piles on the floor, and several bundles covered the tops of two cast iron radiators. Wall-to-wall bookcases, filled beyond capacity, lined two of the walls. Navy and Air Force flags sat on either side of a large leaded glass window directly behind his desk.

"Good morning, chief, sorry I'm late."

Michael glanced at his watch but didn't look up. He took a sip of coffee and motioned for Edward to sit down.

"What's going on with the Air Force project? We have deliverables due in ninety days and a quarterly report due next Friday. The bastards have been on me all morning."

"Yeah, I know. The report's not the problem. It'll be done on time. The real problem is that we don't have anything good to report. We're having problems with the fittings and seal on the main guidance unit in the nose cone. Preliminary tests indicate it's a design flaw, probably means will have to go back to the board and redesign the—"

"Go back to the board! We can't go back to the damn board. We don't have the time. It will tack on an additional six months. Jesus, Edward! You've got to do better. I want you off everything until we're back on track, and that includes Jackson Enterprises."

"Bullshit! I'm not dropping the Jackson contract just because you agreed to move up the friggin' deadlines. I'll walk before I allow you to do that. And I don't appreciate being talked to like some kiss-ass flunky who's here at your beck and call. The original contract deadline with the Air Force is six months away. Remember? We built in time for troubleshooting and design problems like this. You can't rush some of this shit, and you have to expect mistakes along the way. The military's great for moving deadlines up. The bastards don't give a damn about the consequences. You agreed to it. I didn't! I warned you that we'd have problems."

Michael stared coldly at Edward, and struggled to remain in control. He stood up after a moment and walked to the window. "Can we run tests on the guidance system with the current fittings and seal while we redesign them? That way we'll be able to test some of the other components, and hopefully it will give us something favorable to report."

"Sure, but we're going to have to repeat those tests with the new fittings and seal so it's not going to buy us any real time. We're still looking at another six months for completion."

"Good! Then do it. I don't want any mention of the design flaw in the report. Okay?" Michael said, still staring out the window.

Edward raised an eyebrow and shook his head. He thought about disagreeing but decided it wasn't worth the effort. Even if he included the data in his report, Michael would delete it and submit a revised copy to the Air Force anyway. "Yeah, sure, I won't mention it at all. What reason are you going to give for the delay?"

"Don't worry about it. That's my problem. Just run the tests and get the report to me. I'll deal with Major Adams myself. That is, if he pulls his head out of his ass long enough to listen." Michael pulled himself away from the window and sat back down at his desk. "Now fill me in on the Navy contract."

Edward pulled a copy of his handwritten progress notes from a manilla folder and tossed them on the desk. "We're making excellent progress. The wind tunnel tests and firing sequences have gone off without a hitch. We're preparing for several underwater runs before we field test the entire system. Everything looks good so far. It's a tight time-frame but I think we'll squeak in just under the wire."

"Good, can you prepare a formal report by the first of the month?"

"It's already half done. You'll have it on your desk early next week."

Michael nodded and forced a smile. "That should do it for now. I've got a board meeting at nine-thirty and I need to make a few calls first," he said, glancing at his watch again.

"I want to fill you in on the Jackson project before you go. I've made some significant—"

"It will have to wait. I don't have the time this morning. Why don't you write a report and give it to Norma? I'll get to it when I get a chance," Michael interrupted. "I'll talk with you later. I've really got to run." He buzzed Norma on the intercom and asked her to get Major Adams on the phone while Edward put his papers back in order, grabbed his coat and headed out the door. Michael never looked up or said goodbye. Instead, he buried his face in the pile of papers on his desk and took another sip of coffee.

*   *   *

Edward's research at the University of Buffalo was becoming more demanding and the pressure to produce more intense. His research on missile guidance systems was a full decade ahead of anyone else. The military, anxious to put its failures in Korea behind it, was desperately seeking an advantage in the Cold War with the Soviets. Deadlines were moved up, with financial windfalls and future lucrative contracts used as incentives. Michael Anderson had overextended the department's resources. Making promises he couldn't possibly keep. Ultimately, Edward would pay the price. He had been the best man at Edward's wedding and was his son's godfather, but the stress had driven a wedge between the two. Edward knew he'd have to leave soon. Oddly, it was a small, seemingly insignificant contract with a local research company that kept him at the university.

Jackson Enterprises was a year-old, privately funded, research and development company specializing in new fuel technology. Its contract with UB, a twenty-five thousand-dollar grant to determine the theoretical feasibility of utilizing hydrogen as a fuel source, was the company's only outside contract.

Edward had made significant progress on the project and felt he wasn't far from a major breakthrough. If successful, his work had the potential to revolutionize virtually every type of fuel powered system in existence. The applications would be limitless and the financial windfall, astronomical.

Hydrogen, one of the world's most abundant and inexpensive elements, is also one of the most volatile; especially when pressurized and exposed to heat. Both conditions would be necessary for any practical applications.

Gregory Jackson, the company's owner and founder, had several preliminary discussions with Edward regarding employment with his firm. The discussions were more exploratory than substantive at first. Edward had already decided that if the right offer was put on the table, he'd accept.

   *   *   *

Edward was balancing a hot cup of coffee in one hand, his briefcase and coat in the other as he fumbled with his keys, all while squeezing a half-eaten apple between his teeth. He managed to slide the key into the lock without spilling too much of the coffee. The key slid neatly in, but wouldn't turn. After a few errant tries he removed the key, checked it, and tried again, still without success. Finally, after a few more attempts he forced the key and tripped the lock.

"Christ! What the hell's wrong with the lock? That's never happened before." He tossed his briefcase on the desk. "I'll have to call mainte-nance and have them look at it."

He sat down, emptied his briefcase, leaned back in his chair, and reflected on his meeting with Michael. He realized that he was more dis-appointed than angry. There had been too many skirmishes lately, and he was at a point where they didn't bother him that much anymore. Not like they used to, and that's when he knew it was time to leave. He leaned forward and reached for the phone.

"Hi, honey, it's me. How's everything?"

"Oh, not too much different from when you left a little over an hour ago. Your son's been in the driveway all morning playing catch with the pitch-back. He said you promised to take him to the park after dinner."

Edward laughed. "Yep, that's the plan. Do you want to come too?"

"You sure you won't mind if I tag along with the boys?"

"I suppose we can make an exception this time. Just don't expect to *tag* along every time. I should be home by six."

"We'll be ready, Eddie!" There was a long pause as she waited for a response. She spoke up when one didn't come. "You didn't call just to see how we're doing. Did you? How did your meeting with Michael go?"

"You really do know me. Don't you? I'd like to talk about it later if we could. I think it might be time to move on. I don't look forward to com-ing to work anymore and that's not like me."

"To tell you the truth, I'm surprised you lasted this long."

"Maybe it's time for a fresh start. I'd like to leave UB after a few of the contracts are wrapped up. That way, I'm not leaving Michael hanging. I was wondering if we could invite Greg Jackson and his wife over for dinner within the next few weeks. What do you think?"

"Next Saturday would work out well. Let's talk about it tonight. You can call Greg and see if they're free."

"Sounds good. I know he can't afford to pay me as much as UB, but I'm closing in on something that could really turn the company around. I'm just a step away from it. I can feel it. If it works, it will be big. Really big!"

"Hey! You don't have to convince me. I'm already sold. Things might be tight for a while but we'll manage. God knows I didn't marry you for your money."

"Sometimes I wonder why you did marry me."

"So do I. Now get back to work so you can get home on time. Okay?"

"I will. Give Rob a hug and kiss for me. Will you? Oh, Helen, I almost forgot. Have you noticed any problems with our phone? It seemed to take a few extra seconds to connect and I heard a couple of strange clicks."

"I hadn't noticed anything but I really wasn't paying attention."

"It's probably nothing. The phone system here is pretty lame. Some wires probably got crossed or something. Let me know if you notice anything, though. I'll have to call the phone company if it's on our end."

"I'll keep my ears peeled, so to speak," Helen quipped.

"Sounds good. No pun intended. See you later."

✳   ✳   ✳

Edward's pace was somewhere between walking and jogging as he cruised through the building after lunch. He was hurrying back for a conference call and was approaching his office when a fat, balding man suddenly rounded the corner and collided with him. Both men tumbled to the floor. A brown leather satchel slid across the polished linoleum, crashing against the wall and spilling its contents across the floor. Edward managed to get to his feet first and extended a hand to the stranger. After a brief moment of indecisiveness, the man reluctantly accepted the assistance and was pulled to his feet.

"I umm…I'm a…sorry I ran into you, I hope you're all right. It's entirely my fault, I'm afraid I wasn't paying attention to where I was going," the man said, brushing off his pants. His navy blue sport coat was a size and a half too small, and the tire around his waist stretched his white cotton shirt to the brink of splitting. A thin, plaid, clip-on tie rolled down over his flabby chest, coming to rest a good six inches short of his belt. His beige knit pants, at least two inches too long, were badly wrinkled. Both knees were lightly soiled.

"I'm fine. How about you?" Edward asked.

"Everything seems to be in working order," the man commented without looking up. His high-pitched voice and southern drawl didn't match his looks. "I must have got turned around and lost my sense of direction. I was looking for the exit."

"It's back there, just around the corner. Here, let me help you with your things," Edward said, bending over and reaching toward the items scattered across the floor.

"No!" the man yelled, grabbing hold of Edward's arm. "That won't be necessary. I'm sure you have more important matters to attend to, Professor. I'll clean up." He didn't release his grip until Edward pulled his arm back.

Paolucci shrugged his shoulders. "If you insist. Have a good day."

"Thank you, and the same to you."

Edward walked past him and nodded. As he turned the corner, he noticed a small roll of electrical tape on the floor just outside his office. "Hey! This must be yours too," he yelled, picking up the tape and tossing it to the stranger.

"Uhh…yes, I believe it is. Thanks again, doc."

Edward waved but didn't say a word. He turned around and disappeared inside his office. *That's odd. I wonder how he knew I was a professor?* he thought as he closed the door behind him. He took off his coat, sat down at his desk and the telephone rang before he could give it a second thought.

If the window shades hadn't been drawn, he might have noticed the stranger climb into the passenger seat of a black convertible parked in the lot behind his office. The driver finished his cigarette, flipped the butt out the window and slowly pulled away, leaving a pile of spent cigarettes behind. "Did you finish?" he asked.

The fat man looked away, wiping the sweat from his forehead. "Yeah. We're set. They're all in place," he said quietly, deciding not to volunteer any information about his encounter with Paolucci.

CHAPTER 3

"It's beautiful out here, isn't it?" Jenna Jackson said to her husband as they drove south on Seneca Street. One-hundred-year-old maple trees lined the winding, rolling country road. Sunlight ricocheted from tree to tree, flooding the holes between their reddish-orange leaves. Small picturesque farms, set hundreds of yards back from the road, remained as they had for half a century. Mile upon mile of barbed-wire fencing kept cattle from wandering onto the road.

"It's hard to believe that we're less than a half an hour outside the city. I bet we haven't seen a soul for the last ten miles. It's been so long since we were in the country that I almost forgot how peaceful and relaxing it can be. God, what I wouldn't give to own a couple of horses again," Greg Jackson said. "There's the circle Edward described. You'd better wake Brett up. We'll be there in a few minutes. He's been sleeping the whole way here. Is he feeling okay?"

"He's fine. He got up earlier than usual this morning," she answered, reaching back and gently shaking her son. "Robert's Brett's age, isn't he?"

"Yep. I bet two of them will get along like two peas in a pod. Let's see…turn left on Prospect Avenue. Second house on the left. Here we are," Greg said, crunching the directions and tossing them on the floor. "Yes sir. Right on time. Not bad timing, if I do say so myself."

*   *   *

Greg Jackson and his family had moved from Houston to Buffalo. Their southern dialect was unmistakable, but Brett's drawl had already begun to fade. Seven years earlier, Greg's father and uncle had founded Lone Star Oil Inc., which rapidly grew to be the largest and most lucrative oil refinery in Texas.

Everything was going well until an accident on an offshore rig in the Gulf. Their largest rig had been closed for repairs to its main crane. Greg's father, Jeb, was concerned about a massive gulf storm that was heading inland. He thought there would be extensive damage to the rig if the crane wasn't secured properly. So he and his brother, Daniel, headed out to the rig late at night. A half hour after they arrived, a suspicious explosion hurled Jeb's body into the churning sea. By the time the Coast Guard picked up Daniel's call on their radio, and deciphered the words between his sobs, Jeb's body had already been swept far out to sea. An extensive search failed to turn up any sign of Greg's father and he was presumed dead by week's end. A subsequent investigation identified a spark from an acetylene torch as the likely cause of the explosion. The death was ruled accidental.

Daniel Jackson wasted little time mourning his older brother's death. As Greg and his mother grieved, he positioned himself legally, quickly forced them out, and bought their share of the company for a fraction of its worth.

Greg and his wife had enough. A year and a half of legal wrangling and mounting attorney fees got the better of them. So, they decided to cut their losses and head north.

*   *   *

"The kids seem to be hitting it off," Greg said.

"They sure do. It doesn't take much. Does it? A couple of airplanes, tanks, and a sandbox," Edward replied.

"Yeah, too bad life doesn't stay so simple. God! It's really quiet out here. It makes me realize just how much I miss the country."

"We like it. The drive can be a little long, especially in the winter, but it's worth it. There's a quaintness here that you don't find in the city anymore. We sort of stumbled on the place. Helen and I were dating at the time, and we decided to go for a ride to pick apples on a small farm about ten miles south of here. We got lost on the way home and turned down this street by mistake. We noticed the 'For Sale' sign, and the rest is history. How about if we take the kids to the park after dinner? It's only a few blocks away. I'm sure Brett would have a ball there."

*   *   *

"Can I help with anything?" Jenna Jackson asked.

"Would you ask my husband to get the grill going? He hates to cook but loves grilling. You'd think he was a kid lighting his first campfire. He's very precise in setting the newspaper under the charcoal in just the right pattern and thickness. Sprinkling the right amount of lighter fluid in just the right places and lighting all four corners of the paper. In clockwise order of course. It's the funniest thing."

Jenna laughed, swung the back screen door open and stepped out onto the patio. "Helen would like you to get the grill started," she yelled.

Edward nodded and waved. "Come on, Greg, let's go to the patio."

"Try not to burn the house down this time," Helen yelled from the kitchen.

"Very funny. Very funny. Just have those T- Bones ready 'cause Chef Edwardo has arrived."

"Don't worry, Helen, I'll man the fire extinguisher just in case," Greg teased.

"You know you're good when all you need is one match," Edward boasted, striking a blue tip on the side of the house and lighting a corner of the newspaper. "Believe it or not, I did an analysis of the most efficient way to position the charcoal for an even burning fire."

"Are you serious?"

"Sure am. Actually, it was easier to analyze than I thought it would be. I found that it's not so much the position of the charcoal that matters, but rather the angle they lay. If you tilt them approximately twelve degrees, you get the most efficient heat possible. Just enough air flows around the bottom of the charcoal to fuel the fire. Although, to be perfectly honest, it's not all that more efficient than just pouring them right out of the bag and leaving them where they land. That's what I did here, but don't tell Helen. She still thinks I'm crazy enough to place them in the grill one at a time."

They both laughed, watched the fire rise through the steel grill, and drank a cold beer.

"What do you think about the presidential election?" Greg asked, tossing his empty can in the trash.

"I'm not really sure yet. I haven't made up my mind. Nixon has a hell of a lot more experience. I don't really know much about Kennedy, but I trust him. I like him and I'm at a loss to tell you why. I was surprised when he beat Humphrey in the primary."

"My vote's with Kennedy. I'm tired of hearing all the rhetoric from Nixon and the Republicans. A whole lot of talk with no action."

"I'm looking forward to their debate. It'll be interesting to see how Kennedy holds up under fire," Edward said, lifting two cans of beer from the cooler and tossing one to Greg. "Here you go. Just what the doctor ordered."

"Thanks. I heard Kennedy's planning a stop in Buffalo before Election Day."

"Yeah, I heard the same thing. I bet Nixon won't be far behind."

"Hey, honey, is the fire ready yet? We've got some pretty hungry kids here," Helen yelled.

"We're ready. Bring on the T-bones."

＊　　　　＊　　　　＊

After dinner, Edward and Greg took the boys to the park. Brett and Robert played on the slides and swings while their fathers looked on from a nearby picnic table.

"I'm thinking of leaving UB and wanted to discuss working for Jackson Enterprises full-time. I need some time to wrap up a few things and tie up a few loose ends, all in all it should take a month. Maybe less."

"I can't afford to pay you close to what you're making at UB, but I'm willing to throw in some incentives. I definitely want you working for my company. I'm prepared to do whatever it takes to bring you here."

"We're really close to something big. So close I can taste it. Most of the theoretical work's been completed and we should be ready for practical application tests by the end of the year. I've developed a model which should address all of the compression and combustion difficulties. The real sticking point will be in the storage area. I still have a few theoretical applications to resolve around supercooling the gas and storing it as a liquid. I can get it to the right temperature, but I'm not sure how to hold it there yet. Still, I think fossil fuels will be obsolete within a few years. The entire industry will become extinct and Jackson Enterprises will hold the only patent for the hydrogen fuel system."

"God! That would be something. Wouldn't it? I've grown up with oil all my life. I remember my dad taking me out to the oil fields day after day. I'll never forget the smell of crude as it's pumped from the ground. You can't escape the stench. It permeates everything; your clothes, hair, even your skin. It takes days for the odor to leave you." Greg's eyes narrowed and he unconsciously clenched his fists. "I hated everything about oil. From the fields full of mud to the men who worked them. They were as crude as the oil they pumped. Spending a week's pay in company bars and whore houses, and beating the shit out of their wives if they dared to complain. But I kept working there with my father anyway. I was too afraid to tell him how I really felt, and he was too afraid to ask. Everything he did was for me and I fought like hell to hang onto the business when he died."

Greg stood up, picked up a small rock, aimed at a brown squirrel about twenty yards away and let it fly. The squirrel dropped the acorn he was stuffing into his mouth and scurried up the closest tree as the rock skidded to a halt about two feet in front of him. "I don't know what really happened the day my dad died on the offshore rig. But I know it wasn't an accident, he was too careful. He always lectured me about being careful and taking precautions. My uncle murdered him just as sure as I'm standing here. I don't have any proof but I know it in my heart."

He picked up another rock and slowly rolled it back and forth between his fingers and palm. "It all fell apart after Dad died. My uncle robbed us blind and I couldn't do a thing about it. He took everything Mom and Dad worked so hard to get." Greg paused, looked at Brett and continued. "I don't give a rat's ass about the oil business. I never have. It was my father's dream. Not mine. I know that nothing I do will change the past. It sure as hell won't bring him back, but it might help to set things right again and that's all I'm looking to do. I want to watch my uncle's empire crumble all around him, leaving him penniless and impotent."

He tossed the small rock on the ground and sat down, letting his feet dangle off the edge of the table. "I'm willing to offer you fifty percent of the company. You'll be an equal partner. I'll supply the capital. You supply the brains," he said, extending his hand across the table. "What do you say? Is it a deal?"

Edward smiled and shook his hand. "You've got yourself a deal, partner."

"Great, I'll have the papers drawn up by week's end."

"There's no need to hurry."

"The sooner we get started, the better," Greg said. "We'll make one hell of a team."

"You know, Greg, there is one thing I want to tell you now that *we've* reached an agreement."

"Yeah. What is it?"

"I would have settled for twenty-five percent."

Greg laughed. "Make sure you read the fine print in the papers my lawyers draw up. You know, I could have hit that squirrel with the rock if I wanted to. I was a hell of a pitcher in high school."

"I don't care how good a pitcher you were. There's no way you would hit the bastard. Here take this rock and let 'er rip. I'll bet fifty percent of *our* company that you miss him clean."

"Too late, the kids are coming. I wouldn't want to set a bad example," Greg said, tossing the rock to the ground and laughing.

CHAPTER 4

October 1960

The 1960 presidential election was winding down and all of the major polls showed a dead heat between Kennedy and Nixon, with less than a month of campaigning left. Their televised debate, the first ever, was considered a draw and left the candidates scrambling for an edge. New York, critical to both parties, was still too close to call. Both candidates planned several stops in key cities in the state, and Buffalo was on the short list.

*   *   *

The national physics convention was scheduled for late October in Massachusetts, and would afford Edward his last opportunity to present a paper on behalf of the university. He booked the last remaining seat on a twin engine, nonstop commuter flight between Buffalo and Boston.

His research at Jackson Enterprises continued, mostly in the evenings and on weekends, because of the enormous amount of time he was devoting to tying up all of the loose ends at UB. None of his work was published, and wouldn't be until all phases of the project were completed and patents obtained. It was hard for him to adjust to the private sector at first. He would have already published several preliminary articles if this had been a research project at the university. But the objectives were different now, his research was kept under lock and key and only he and Greg had access to it. The level of secrecy was foreign to him and unfortunately, he didn't adjust to the change quickly enough. He wasn't a suspicious person by nature. Perhaps if he had been, he would have noticed the faint glow of a cigarette, coming from a black convertible which had been parked on a side street adjacent to his new office for three nights in a row. He never noticed the car, the broken streetlight above it, or the slight click when he used the phone.

*   *   *

It was a little after 10:00 P.M., and Edward was working alone in his lab the night before his trip to Boston. He had skipped dinner, gone straight to the lab from UB, and worked uninterrupted with the exception of Helen's phone call at 7:00 P.M.

"Holy shit! That's it!" he yelled, leaping to his feet and thrusting a fist in the air. "It works. It friggin' works! I don't believe it." He anxiously paced around the room trying to think of things he could have missed. Reasons it shouldn't work. He checked and rechecked his calculations but the numbers kept adding up the same. He knew he hadn't missed anything. He knew he was right.

He snatched the Rolodex off his desk, spun it to the card with Greg's home phone number, picked up the phone and dialed. There was a click and a short pause a split second before the phone rang. The fat man sitting in the passenger seat of the black convertible tossed his crossword puzzle down, turned the tape recorder on and adjusted his headphones.

"Hey Greg, it's me. Sorry to call so late but, we did it! We really did it! We can cool hydrogen to a liquid and hold it for as long as we want. In other words, we're in business, partner!"

"Yeeeeeeee Haaw!" Greg yelled in his usual slow southern drawl. "Where the hell are you?"

"At the lab."

"Stay put. I'll be there in two shakes of a lamb's tail."

"Sorry, but I can't. I've got to get home. Helen's going to kick my ass, I haven't been home yet and I have a nine-forty-five flight to Boston tomorrow night. How about if I close up here and call you in the morning? There are a few minor details that need to be worked out but nothing too difficult. Just some fine tuning, that's all. I'll be able to work on them in Boston and we should be ready to roll when I get back. Let's plan on meeting Tuesday morning here at the lab. Okay?"

"How about if I take you to the airport? We'll stop for a cup of coffee or something. That way we can talk before you leave. I'll pick you up at eight-thirty. Okay?"

"Sure, if you're buying," Edward joked.

"Don't worry, I'll pick up the tab. I'll even throw in a doughnut. We're really going to be able to do it! Aren't we?"

"You bet. Nothing can stop us now."

"Hey, you better get home to Helen before she kills you."

"I know. I'm just about outta here. I'll call you in the morning."

"Good enough, I'll talk with you—oh! One more thing."

"Yeah."

"Thanks. Thanks for everything, Edward."

"Hey, I couldn't have done it without you. Now get some sleep and I'll call you in the morning."

"Talk with you then," Greg said.

Edward hung up and tried calling home. He didn't get a dial tone at first. Just static.

"Greg, is that you?" he asked.

A second of silence was followed by a click and a dial tone. He dialed his home phone number again without giving it a second thought.

"Honey. It's me. I'm on my way home and I've got great news. Why don't you chill that bottle of champagne we've been saving for a special occasion?"

"Why, what happened? What's going on?"

"I'll tell you when I see you. I love you. See you soon, bye."

A few moments after he hung up the phone, the black convertible pulled away from the curb with its lights out. Glass from the broken streetlight lay untouched on the tree lawn. The faint outline of two men reflected through the windshield as it passed under a neon sign and turned the corner heading north on Delaware Avenue.

One day later

"Are you sure you have everything?" Helen asked, as she watched her husband toss his luggage on the sofa.

"It's not like I'm going away for a week, honey. I'll be back in a day and a half."

"That's what you said the last time you went out of town, and you ended up forgetting to pack a single pair of dress pants. You had to wear the same pair of jeans all week. Remember?"

Edward laughed. "Hey, we all make mistakes. You should have seen the look on Michael's face when I showed up at the meeting in a pair of Levi's. Boy! That was something. I wish I had a camera that day."

"Hey, Dad, are you going to bring me back anything from Boston?" Robert asked, tugging on his father's coat.

Edward scooped up his son and hoisted him onto his shoulders. "What would you like?"

"Could you get me an erector set? I saw this neat one on TV. It even has a 'lectric motor so you can make cars and cranes and other neat stuff."

"Hmm, what do you think, Mom? Do you think Boston would have something like that?"

"I suppose so. Just for good boys though!"

Robert's eyes were wide and he had a smile from ear-to-ear.

"You promise to take care of your Mother while I'm gone. You're the man of the house until I get back. Okay?"

"I'll take good care of Mommy while you're in Boston."

"Good. I knew I could count on you. Now slide down here and give me a great big hippo hug!"

The doorbell rang a second later. Edward glanced at his watch. "That must be Greg, right on time as usual." He picked up his briefcase and luggage, kissed Helen and Robert goodbye, and walked to the door. "I'll call you from Boston. I should get in about eleven-thirty."

Helen watched her husband walk out the door and climb into Greg's car. It would turn out to be the last time she would see him alive.

*   *   *

Light from the car's headlights swept through the living room, reflecting off the far wall, as the car slowly pulled into the driveway. Helen was engulfed by the leather recliner, sound asleep, the latest Hitchcock novel resting in her lap. Robert was curled up on the sofa, clutching his baseball glove. Last month's Spiderman comic book lay on the floor below his head. Neither heard the car door close, the sound of footsteps on the porch, or the first knock at the door. The second knock, much more deliberate than the first, startled her. A few seconds passed before the cobwebs cleared and she stumbled to the front door.

Edward's flight must have been canceled and he's locked himself out, she thought, just before opening the door.

Michael Anderson stood alone on the front porch looking more distressed than Helen ever remembered seeing him. The soft glow of the porch light illuminated the paleness and pain in his face. Tears streaked down his cheeks, cascading onto the collar of his trench coat. His voice cracked badly as he struggled to speak.

"Michael! What's wrong? What are you doing here?" she asked anxiously.

He stared at her for a moment before closing his eyes and turning away. He pinched the bridge of his nose and wiped the tears from his face. He stammered at first, desperately searching for the right words. Finally, he collected himself long enough to speak.

"I just heard on the radio that the nine-forty-five flight to Boston...Edward's plane, it...umm...it went down somewhere over the Appalachians. There weren't any survivors. I'm sorry, Helen, but he's gone. Edward's dead. I'm so sorry. So damn—"

"No!" she screamed. "No, it's not true. You're wrong, Michael. You must have got the flight numbers mixed up. It's not true," she cried, pounding his chest with her fists. "He's going to call any minute now. He promised he would call. You'll see. He'll call. Please, dear God. Don't let it be true!"

*   *   *

Robert's world exploded in the blink of an eye. Half of all he was and all he knew died on the frigid snow-covered ridges of the Appalachians. Childhood dreams and the innocence of youth lay scattered among the twisted, burning wreckage of Flight 687.

CHAPTER 5

1983

Willie swung the cage door open and slowly stepped onto the cold, sterile laboratory table. Still groggy from anesthesia, and more cautious than usual, he wandered across the black tabletop, coming to rest a couple of feet from its beveled edge. He stood still. Shook his head from side to side and reached for a large, peeled banana sitting alone in a green bowl. After carefully sniffing it and looking over his shoulder, the chimpanzee popped it in his mouth, took a few bites, and swallowed.

"Well it's about time, Willie. I thought you'd never wake up. I was starting to worry. How's that arm feeling, little fella? The incision's intradermal so it shouldn't be too sore," Dr. Robert Paolucci said, glancing up from his microscope. "Come here and let me have a look."

He examined the small circular incision on the chimp's forearm, carefully inspecting the tiny sutures.

"Hmm…looks pretty damn good if I do say so myself. Don't worry. You'll be no worse for the wear. Now let's test that fancy new biochip I tucked away in there while you were knocked out."

It took a few minutes for the laptop to boot-up, and about half as long to load the software. Willie climbed into Robert's lap, snatched his Yankee's baseball cap from his head, and played with the collection of

25

pencils cluttering his front pocket. "Okay, Willie, that should just about do it," he said as he slipped a cuff over the chimp's forearm.

He hit a few buttons on the keyboard and watched the blank blue screen fill up with a smorgasbord of tables and graphs.

"Hot damn, it works! Now let's check out your vitals; blood pressure looks good, heart rate's a little elevated but that's probably due to the anesthesia…nothing to worry about. EKG looks normal. Let's find out about your blood gases," he said, sliding the mouse a few inches to the left and clicking. "Hmm…they look pretty good. Bet a lot of chimps wished they had blood gases that looked this good. Now hold still, I'm going to run a CBC differential. Hold it. Hold it. Atta boy, just a few more seconds…done!"

"Good-boy, Willie. Now all I have to do is print the data, copy it over to the hard drive, and we're set. A few more runs over the next couple of weeks and we'll be ready to send you back."

The phone rang and Willie jumped, leaping into Robert's arms.

"I can't believe you're *still* there. Your dinner's been ready for half an hour. Honestly, you remind me more of your father each day. Do you know how many times I had to call to remind him about dinner?" Helen Paolucci said.

"More times than Carter has liver pills I bet," Robert teased.

"Your sense of humor's as bad as your father's was, now please get in your car and head home. Now!"

"Sure thing, Mom. I'll be there in twenty-five minutes. Oh, by the way, would you mind if I brought Willie along? He's a little groggy and I'd like to keep an eye on him tonight."

"I suppose so, just keep him away from the cat. Comet goes crazy every time Willie's here. It takes a week before he's back to normal."

"Don't worry, I'll keep an eye on him. I promise. Thanks, Mom, you're the best. See you soon."

   *   *   *

Helen Paolucci slid a bookmark into her novel and tossed it onto the coffee table when she heard her son's car pull into the driveway. Willie raced up the porch steps, caught sight of the cat, and scooted past her just as she opened the screen door. All Robert saw was the back of Comet's legs sliding out from under him as he scurried around the corner. Willie was a few yards behind but closing fast.

"Willie, leave the cat alone!" his mother screamed.

Robert shook his head and tossed his bags on the porch. "Oops!" he said as he sprinted passed his mother.

When he entered the kitchen, he found the cat on top of the refrigerator, squeezed underneath the cabinets, hair on end and hissing. Willie stood on the counter, poised to make a leap to the top of the refrigerator.

"Hold it right there, Willie. Get down from there. Now!" he ordered.

Willie hesitated for a moment, glaring at Comet one last time before jumping down to the floor.

"I thought he was groggy," Helen said, entering the kitchen. "We're just about ready to eat. You take care of Cheetah and get the poor cat down. Look at him. He's scared stiff. He'll probably need counseling."

*   *   *

Robert had barely begun to cut his steak when his mother started in on him.

"How's Anne doing?" she asked.

"Okay I guess. I've been pretty busy lately."

Helen filled her wine glass and took a short sip. "She's been patient, but she's not going to wait forever, you know. You have to decide what is more important to you because it's not fair to her. You've been dating for five years and sometimes I think you take her for granted. Besides, you're not getting any younger. Don't you think it's about time?"

"How did Dad manage to do it? How did he spend all that time at UB and still have time for us? How the hell did he fit it all in?"

"It wasn't easy but somehow he did. I'm not saying he never came home late or worked weekends. Because he did. But he always managed to be there when it counted. Do you remember all of the times he would wake you up early in the morning, before sunrise, and take you for a walk? He knew he wouldn't be home before you went to bed so he made sure he spent time with you when he could. It was the little things he did to try and make up for the long hours at work. The long hours away from you."

Robert looked past his mother at the picture of his father that sat on the dining room hutch. "I wish I could remember. I can't tell you how many times I've tried to remember something about him, but I can't. Not anymore, there's nothing there. At least you have memories to hold on to. I don't. I wish to God that I did, but all I have are faded photographs. Nothing else." He got up, picked up the picture and sat down at the table again. "What if it were possible to step back into time," he said, turning the photo toward her. "To the moment this picture was taken. To stay long enough to see him. To talk with him. One last chance to hold him again. What would you do? Would you go back to see him? Would you take the chance, even if you might not be able to get back home again?"

Helen took the picture from him and stared at it for a moment, rubbing her fingers over her husband's face. "Even after all of these years, there isn't a day that goes by that I don't think about him. I still love him. I still miss him and I wish he was here with us. I'd give anything for that. I'm sorry you can't remember. I wish you could. But sometimes remembering makes it harder. Sometimes it's better not to remember, because then you don't hurt as much."

Helen put the photo down on the table and looked up, tears rolled down her cheeks. "Yes, I'd step back in time to see him one last time, if I could. I'd give anything to be able to hold him again and tell him how much I love him. I'd take that chance."

Four weeks later

Willie sat on the bed and quietly played with his colored building blocks while Robert made a few final adjustments to the computer program. Books, papers, and an assortment of computer equipment covered his desk. A faded black and white photograph of himself riding a bicycle acted as a bookmark for his journal. The handwritten date of May 7, 1960 was scrawled diagonally across its back.

A cable from the computer's serial port was connected to a plastic, rectangular shaped black box, similar in size to a shoe box. It was opaque and completely encased except for a small aperture, a quarter-inch in diameter, located on its far side. The box was positioned approximately two feet from the end of the desk, and a three foot square metal cage sat on a small table directly across from it.

Robert slid the mouse across the pad, dragging the arrow down the menu list to the Open command, and clicked. The hard drive hummed. A red light on the box blinked and a panel on its top slid open, exposing its interior. The box was lined with a lead alloy and the side closest to the computer was jammed full of microprocessors. A miniature high intensity laser sat in the middle of the box, directly in front of a paper thin platinum bracket which was sandwiched by high index refractive lenses. The lens on the far end of the bracket was attached to a four-inch, red, metallic cylinder which terminated at the exterior aperture.

Robert picked up the photograph and checked the date on the back before slipping it between the two lenses. He made a few minor adjustments then dragged the arrow down and clicked on the Close command. There was a pause, and the hard drive hummed again, followed by a few more clicking noises. The red light blinked and the panel on top of the box slid closed a second later.

"That should just about do it. Everything's ready, Willie."

Willie stared, scratched the top of his head, and continued playing with the blocks.

"Yeah, I know you don't know what's going on. To be honest with you, I'm not completely sure myself. But if everything goes the way I'm expecting, you'll be all grown-up the next time I see you. I'm sure going to miss you. The truth is, I wouldn't be able to keep you much longer anyway. Don't worry. They'll take good care of you at the zoo. We've been quite a team though, haven't we?" Robert said, stuffing the equipment into a large duffle bag. "Well I guess it's time, you'll be fine. I promise." He hugged Willie, put him in the cage and locked the door. The steel cage was empty except for an old metal 'Gunsmoke' lunch box filled with two bananas, a few homemade chocolate chip cookies and a handwritten note which read:

> *Please take good care of me. My name is Willie, I'm a five-year-old chimpanzee, and I'm looking for a good home. Would you please take me to the Buffalo Zoo?*
>
> *P.S. My favorite desert is coconut cream pie!*

Robert swung the duffle bag over his shoulder, picked up the cage and headed to Hamlin park. Halfway through the park, Willie slid his long arm through the cage door and swiped the Yankee's baseball cap from Robert's back pocket.

Robert shook his head and laughed. "All right, I suppose you can take it with you. It shouldn't get in the way."

Willie grinned, put the cap on his head, and enjoyed the remainder of the ride. They came upon a small clearing surrounded by chestnut trees and thick shrubs on the southeast side of the park, less than a hundred yards from the swings. Nearby, a small brook wove its way through tangled shrubs and spilled into a shallow pond that was home to a family of ducks.

"This looks as good of a place as any," Robert said, laying the duffle bag on a tree stump and the cage on the grass. He placed the cage on the edge of a four-by-six-foot blue rubber mat, and carefully measured the distance between the end of the black box and the cage. He slowly inched the box forward until it was exactly two feet away. He attached one end of an electrode to Willie's forearm, the other end to the serial port, and ran a few system checks. Confident that everything was working, he slid the arrow down to the start icon. "Take care of yourself, Willie. Have a great life," he said, reaching through the steel bars and holding him one last time. "See you in a couple of decades."

Willie took the baseball cap off and offered it to Robert.

"No. You keep it," he said, pushing his arm back through the bars, letting go and clicking on the mouse. "Goodbye, Willie. Don't forget me."

The red light blinked and the hard drive hummed. A high pitched, piercing noise followed seconds later, resonating off the surrounding trees. A brilliant reddish-orange light shot out of the black box and completely illuminated the cage. The brightness of the eerie light forced Robert's eyes closed and by the time he opened them, the cage, lunch box, and Willie were gone. All that remained was the electrode and blue rubber mat. A dull burnt odor lingered in the air for a moment before the wind carried it away. Fifty feet above the ground, a squirrel sitting on its hind legs, raised his nose to the air and quickly scurried back into its nest.

Robert sat on the grass, staring at the blue mat. "Please be all right." He ran his fingers through his hair, made a couple of keystrokes on the laptop and waited. "Okay, Willie, let's see how you did. Hmm, blood pressure's 163 over 115, heart rate's 122, blood gases look normal although the electrolytes seem a little out of whack. I'll make a complete run when I get back to the lab. But first, I have to get to the library."

        *   *   *

Robert arrived at the library minutes before closing. Ms. Barrister, the evening librarian, wasn't too happy to see him burst through the door with less than thirty minutes left in her work day. She looked every bit the stereotypical librarian, a forty-something spinster with long dark hair pulled back into a tight bun, and thick black plastic rim glasses with coke bottle lenses. She wore a long, black dress with a high button-down collar that had been fashionable a decade and a half earlier. Her puritanical appearance and somber demeanor scared the hell out of any little kid unfortunate enough to speak louder than a whisper on her watch. She was a librarian's librarian in every sense of the word.

"Hello, can you tell me if you have microfiche of the Buffalo Evening News and Courier Express Newspapers dating back to May 1960?" Robert asked, half out of breath.

Ms. Barrister glared at him, looking quite annoyed. She rolled her eyes and let out an audible sigh.

"Microfiche from that long ago would be stored in the back room," she groaned.

A few seconds of silence passed before he realized she had no intentions of retrieving the microfiche.

"Look, ma'am, I know it's late and you probably want to get out of here. But could you please get it for me? I promise I won't be too long. It's very important and means a great deal to me. I really need to look at the film tonight. It can't wait until morning."

Ms. Barrister glanced at her watch, reluctantly nodded, turned without saying a word and headed into the store room.

"Gee, sorry to keep you a few minutes longer. Like you've got a date or something," he whispered.

He could hear the sound of boxes being pulled from shelves and cut open, the rustling of paper, and an occasional grunt. She returned to the desk with two dusty manilla folders a couple of minutes later.

"There are twenty minutes until closing," she said gruffly.

"Great! Thank you very much. I really appreciate it," he said, snatching the folders from her hand.

He had his coat off and was loading the first microfiche into the viewer a half minute later. His face was pressed up against the dimly lit screen as he scanned the table of contents. He anxiously slipped a dozen sheets in and out before finding the Buffalo Evening News Edition from May 8, 1960.

"Come on, come on, it's gotta be here," he repeated, as he scanned through the pages. He had a lump in his throat, and was sick to his stomach as he nervously slid the viewfinder over a few inches at a time, just far enough to land him at the top of the following page. Suddenly he froze. He leaned back in the chair and stared at the screen with his mouth wide open.

The viewfinder was filled with a quarter page photograph of Willie sitting in a steel cage, wearing Robert's Yankees baseball cap. Directly below the photo was an accompanying article whose headline read:

Chimpanzee found abandoned in East Aurora.

The article went on to describe how Zachary Taylor and Tommy Malone, two thirteen-year-old troublemakers, had discovered the chimpanzee in a clearing on the south side of Hamlin Park. The two teenagers, well known for their practical jokes, weren't taken seriously by Tommy's parents at first. Their persistence eventually paid off and Tommy's father reluctantly followed the pair to the park. Within a few minutes, Willie was at Tommy's house, and the police and dog warden were on their way.

"Son-of-a-bitch, it worked! You made it, Willie. It really works."

CHAPTER 6

Two Days Later

"Hello, Dr. Paolucci, please come in, I've been expecting you. Dr. Borelli was called out of town unexpectedly and won't be able to meet with you today. But he asked me to assist you with whatever you needed. I'm Dawn Mackey, the chief veterinarian here at the zoo," she said softly. Her long blond hair was neatly tied back in a ponytail and a stethoscope was draped around her neck. The sleeves on her blue denim shirt were rolled up to the bottom of her elbows, and her jeans were tucked into a pair of brown leather work boots. Robert tried not to stare, but couldn't help himself.

God! She's beautiful, he thought.

"It's nice to meet you, Dr. Mackey," he said, extending his hand.

"Please call me Dawn. Dr. Mackey sounds so pretentious. Every time I hear that name I think of my Dad," she said, nervously tugging on her stethoscope.

"My name's Robert."

"I know. I've heard quite a few stories about you and Dr. Borelli when the two of you were in undergraduate school."

"Don't believe everything he told you. Frank always tended to embellish things quite a bit. As a matter of fact, I wouldn't believe any of it."

"Well I don't know about that," she said, laughing. "Where there's smoke, there's fire."

Robert laughed. "Yeah, Frank usually started them and I usually put them out," he quipped, stepping into the office and closing the door behind him.

"I understand you're conducting research on the aging process in primates."

"Yes, that's correct. My research is currently limited to chimpanzees but I plan on expanding it within the next year. I've been comparing various biological indicators and markers between humans and chimps to see what similarities and differences exist. I'm particularly interested in your older chimps. I have access to newborns at the university but the older ones are hard to come by."

"I'm sure we'll be able to help. We have half a dozen in the fifteen-year-old range, and two that are older than twenty-five."

"Great, can we start with the seniors?"

"We sure can. I'm ready if you are."

Robert swung the backpack over his shoulder and opened the door. "Let's go, I've got everything I need right here in my backpack."

He followed her down three and a half flights of stairs into a subterranean tunnel beneath the zoo. The narrow tunnel was lined with brick and mortar and was less than six feet high. The tunnel was cool, damp, and poorly lit. They walked single file for approximately fifty feet until it split in four directions. Dawn turned down the unmarked tunnel on the far left without hesitating. It was much better lit and seemed slightly newer. There was noticeably less dampness and the air seemed fresher.

"Watch your head," Dawn said, pointing to a small wooden sign hanging from the ceiling by a pair of rusty iron chains. "PRIMATES" was spelled out in large black letters. A faded red arrow pointed straight ahead.

"Here we are," she announced, opening a large wooden door which led to three flights of stairs. The unmistakable sound of chimpanzees screeching and grunting filtered down the stairwell, along with their pungent odor.

Dawn reached the top of the stairs, opened another large door, and stepped inside the primate's quarters. The main room was enormous. Two huge cages, at least 30 feet in height and 60 feet in length, completely covered one of the walls. Each cage contained two steel doors, one opening into the outside habitat, the other into the room. A series of levers, each with a differently colored handle, controlled each of the doors. Cabinets and shelves lined the wall opposite the entrance and a series of exam tables were scattered throughout the shadowy room. Black and brown chimpanzees chased one another back and forth between the outside habitat and the cage, swinging from bars and jumping from perches.

"You never really get used to the smell," Dawn said.

"I would hate to think anyone would," Robert commented, cupping his hand over his nose. "Are the older chimps here?"

Dawn pointed to her left. "Right behind that door. There's an interesting story with the first one we're going to see. All of our chimps were born here at the zoo except for this old-timer. Apparently, he was found abandoned in a park in one of the southtowns more than twenty years ago. They never found his owner and Willie's been with us ever since. He's fathered more than a dozen chimps. He's quite a character." Dawn opened the door and stepped inside the room with Robert close behind. "Unfortunately, he's developed rheumatoid arthritis and hearing loss in the last few years. It's really slowed him down." She reached around the corner and flipped the light switch up. "His eyesight is partially limited due to glaucoma. I really think the illnesses have taken their toll on him. He tends to keep to himself much more than the other chimps. He's definitely introverted with strangers. You'll have trouble getting close to him."

There was a lump in Robert's throat and a burning pain in the pit of his stomach as he stepped through the doorway and saw an aged chimpanzee lying all alone in the corner of a darkened cage. Its back was toward the door, resting against the cold steel bars.

Dawn removed a brass key ring from the near wall, and flipped through half a dozen keys before finding the right one. The pitted, silver key slid cleanly into the keyhole and the lock on the cage door turned easily. Willie didn't hear the jingling of the keys or the creaking of the door. He didn't move at all.

"Willie, wake up, you have company," Dawn said softly.

Willie groaned but didn't wake.

Robert grabbed the back of her arm. "Please, let me," he said, laying his backpack on the floor. He knelt down next to Willie and gently nudged the chimp's shoulder. "Hey, Willie, it's time to rise and shine. Come on, fella, let's get up."

Willie lifted his head. His nostrils strained to absorb more of the scent of the hand that touched him. It was a scent he was familiar with. A scent he struggled to remember. He sniffed and processed, waited, and then sniffed and processed some more. Suddenly, he wailed, sprang to his feet and leapt into Robert's arms, knocking him to the cold cement floor.

Dawn looked on in astonishment. "Do you usually have this effect on chimps? I've never seen him this animated before. If I didn't know better, I'd swear he knows you. It took me more than a month just to get in the same cage with him."

Robert hugged Willie and laughed. "It's good to see you again, Willie," he whispered as the chimp snatched the Yankee's cap from his back pocket. "Maybe I remind him of someone."

"Maybe," Dawn said curiously. "So, you're a Yankee's fan."

"Yep, born and raised. It's one of the few bad habits I inherited from my Dad."

Dawn smiled. "That's a coincidence, Willie was wearing a Yankee's cap the day they found him."

Robert picked the chimp up, held him in his arms and gently stroked his head. "Obviously we're dealing with a highly intelligent animal," he joked. "Well, time to get to work. I don't want to hold you up any longer than necessary." He reached into his backpack and pulled out a few pieces of equipment. "Damn, I forgot my blood pressure cuff. Do you have one I could borrow?"

"Sure, I'll run over to my office and grab one. I'll be back in a flash."

Robert already had the laptop and half of the equipment out before the door closed behind her. He slid a modified blood pressure cuff onto Willie's forearm while waiting for the computer to boot-up.

"Okay, Willie, we're on the clock. Hold still while I look for that fancy biochip of yours."

Robert moved the cuff a few centimeters at a time while looking at the blank monitor. "Where's the chip? It should be right here." The screen remained blank. "Son-of-a-bitch, she'll be back any minute now," he said nervously, glancing back at the door. He could feel sweat forming on his forehead and his heart racing. He was quickly running out of time. Dawn was already at the bottom of the stairwell.

"Come on. Where the hell is it?" He slid the cuff up a few more centimeters. Still nothing but a blank blue screen. "Why can't I find the damn—Shit! I've got the wrong arm. What an idiot. It's a good thing I'm not making rockets!"

He hastily slid the cuff off one arm and onto the other, rotating it until it was positioned on the anterior side of Willie's forearm. "It should be right about here," he said, keeping one eye on the screen and the other on the door. Dawn's approaching footsteps echoed in the stairwell.

Robert shook his head and rotated the cuff a quarter turn. "Damn, not enough time. We'll have to find another way to—" Suddenly rows of data filled the screen. "Sweet Jesus, we hit the motherload! All I need now is a few more seconds to download the—"

The doorknob turned.

"She's back. We're busted."

Dawn was halfway through the door when someone called her name. She stepped back and carried on a conversation in the hallway.

"Come on, Dawn, keep gabbing. All I need is a few more seconds. That's it, keep it coming. Almost there. Done!" Robert hit the Save command, and slid the computer into the backpack just as she entered the room.

Whew! That was close, he thought.

"Here you go," she said, tossing him a blood pressure cuff. "I'm sorry I took so long, but one of our veterinarians had a question about an appendectomy we have scheduled for a polar bear tomorrow morning."

"Not a problem, Willie and I spent the time getting acquainted. Can you tell me what will happen to him when his arthritis gets worse?"

Dawn hesitated and looked away. "There's not a whole lot we can do. We'll medicate him as long as possible to help with the pain, but eventually he'll be put to sleep. As much as I hate to admit it, it comes down to money. It's a lot less expensive to care for a young chimp."

"I'd like to take Willie home with me before that happens. What are my chances?"

"I don't know. I'd have to check with Frank. I don't think he'd object, as long as he wasn't going to be mistreated. I'm certain that wouldn't be the case with you."

"No, you don't have to worry about that. I'd like to study his arthritis and determine if there are any correlations between chimps and humans. He's the perfect age for my research. I'd certainly appreciate it if you'd speak to Frank and let me know."

"Sure, I'd be happy to."

"Thanks," Robert said, rising to his feet. "Well I better get to work. I've got a few chimps to examine, starting with this old-timer."

CHAPTER 7

Dawn Mackey rang the doorbell and stepped back a few feet, nervously clutching Robert's baseball cap, unconsciously wringing it with her hands.

What are you doing here, Dawn? You should have called first, she thought.

The thirty seconds that passed without anyone answering the door seemed like an eternity. She decided against ringing the bell a second time, and slowly retreated down the steps feeling somewhat relieved.

It was a bad idea anyway. I'll call him in the morning, she said to herself.

She was a third of the way down the walkway when Helen Paolucci opened the door and stepped out onto the porch, holding a wet dishrag in one hand. "Can I help you?"

Dawn glanced at the house number above the door and scratched her head. "I'm sorry but I must have the wrong address, I was looking for Dr. Paolucci."

Helen smiled. "You have the right house. Robert's my son. You didn't expect him to still be living with his mother. Did you?"

"To be totally honest with you...no," she said, shaking her head.

"That makes two of us."

Dawn laughed and walked back toward the house, placing a hand on the railing. "I'm Dawn Mackey, a veterinarian at the zoo. Your son stopped by this morning and left his baseball cap. I was headed out this way and thought I'd drop it off."

"He's not at home right now but he should be back soon. He left after dinner, muttered something about the library I think. It's due to close in a half hour or so. Why don't you come inside for awhile? He shouldn't be much longer."

"I don't want to bother you. Are you sure I won't be interrupting something?"

"Nothing at all," Helen said, holding the screen door open. "I could use the company. My son's a heck of a researcher but he's a little short in the recreational conversation department. If you know what I mean."

"I have three brothers. I know exactly what you mean," Dawn quipped, stepping into the living room.

"Can I get you anything to drink? I have a fresh pot of coffee brewing, if you'd like a cup."

"That'd be great."

"Cream and sugar?" Helen asked.

"Just cream, please," Dawn said, walking over to the mantle. She looked at the family photographs while Helen retreated into the kitchen. "Robert's an only child?" she asked.

Helen returned with the coffee, walked to the fireplace and stood next to her. "This picture of my husband was taken just before he left for Boston, the night he died," she said, picking up the black and white photograph.

"We had always planned on having more children but somehow never got around to it. Too busy working, I suppose."

Helen stared at the picture for a moment, cleaned a small fingerprint smudge from the glass and carefully returned it to its spot on the mantle.

"I'm sorry, Mrs. Paolucci, I didn't mean to pry."

"There's nothing to be sorry for. All you did was ask a question. My husband died in a plane crash a long time ago."

Helen looked at Dawn and forced a smile, quickly changing the subject. "By the way, what was my son doing at the zoo?"

"He's involved in research with primates. He wanted to examine a few of our chimpanzees and have blood work run on them. One of the chimps managed to pickpocket his Yankees cap and I wanted to return it to him. So here I am."

"I can never keep up with what he's working on. He's always in the middle of something. I swear he spends more time with Willie than with me. I wouldn't—"

"Willie? Who's Willie?"

"He's a rambunctious five-year-old chimp that Robert has had virtually from the day he was born. He brings him over here every so often, and stays just long enough to drive my cat crazy."

"That's a coincidence. The zoo also has a chimpanzee named Willie. But ours is a lot older. As a matter of fact, Robert saw him this morning. It's strange that he never mentioned anything about his chimp. Do you have a picture of him?"

Helen rummaged through the drawer of the drop leaf table for a minute, before yanking out a photograph of Robert holding Willie on the glider in the backyard. Both were wearing matching Yankees jerseys and caps.

"I guess Willie's a Yankees fan," Dawn noticed.

"It's the strangest thing you've ever seen. He refuses to wear any other team's cap. I guess my son's trained him well. Robert's been a Yankee's fan all his life. Just like his father."

Helen took a sip of coffee and sat back down on the sofa.

Dawn examined the picture one last time before handing it back. A little voice in the back of her head kept telling her that Robert's research had nothing to do with aging. There was something in Willie's file that was bothering her. Something she read when she first came to the zoo. Something that couldn't wait until the morning.

"Well, I suppose I should be going. I have an early start tomorrow. One of our polar bears has an appendicitis that needs surgery. It's scheduled for six and I'm assisting. Thank you so much for the coffee and the visit, I really enjoyed talking with you," Dawn said, getting up and standing next to the sofa.

"You're welcome. Are you sure you can't stay a little longer? He'll probably be home any minute now."

"I'd love to, but I really need to get going."

"Thanks for dropping off the cap. I'll make sure he gets it."

"It was my pleasure. I really enjoyed meeting you and hopefully I'll see you again. Please say hello to your son for me."

*   *   *

Robert fed his last nickel into the copier at just about the same time that Dawn's car was backing out of his mother's driveway.

"Good night, Ms. Barrister," he said as he rushed past the reception desk a couple of minutes later.

The librarian didn't respond or look up. The ends of her lips curled up in a forced smile. Her black trench coat was buttoned up to the collar. A strap from her purse rested on a shoulder. She clutched an umbrella in one hand and set of keys in the other.

He had barely gotten into his car when the lights in the library went out. A few seconds later, Ms. Barrister stepped outside and locked the doors. A single light illuminated the doorway, casting her wiry shadow halfway to the sidewalk. He noticed there weren't any cars in the parking lot and thought about offering her a ride, but couldn't muster the nerve. Instead, he quickly pulled his car ahead and drove out of the parking lot. He glanced in the rearview mirror and watched her lonely silhouette slowly disappear into the shadows.

I should have offered her a ride, he thought.

*   *   *

"Hi Mom, I'm home," Robert announced, stepping off the porch and into the foyer.

"Well it's about time. I wish you had come home about ten minutes ago. A friend of yours stopped by to see you."

"Yeah. Who?"

"Dawn Mackey. She wanted to drop off your Yankees cap. I guess you left it at the zoo today. Actually, I think she's a little sweet on you, and used the hat as an excuse to see you again."

"Now why would you think that? I swear, if a woman so much as glances my way, you think she's looking to marry me. You've got quite an imagination. I think you've been reading too many romance novels, or your estrogen levels are way out of whack. Maybe both! She was probably in the neighborhood, had nothing to do, and decided to drop the hat off. End of story!"

"She didn't just happen to be in the neighborhood and you know it! I'd say you made quite an impression on her today. She's a pretty girl. Seems really nice. I did happen to notice that her ring finger was bare."

Robert shook his head, walked into the kitchen and opened the refrigerator. "So what did the two of you talk about?"

"Mostly about you, she looked at some old photographs and listened to some boring stories. She loved the picture of you and Willie sitting on the glider."

"Why did you show her that picture?" Robert asked. He had a sinking feeling in the pit of his stomach.

"She asked to see one after I mentioned you had a chimp."

Robert ran his fingers through his hair and took a long slow drink from a bottle of beer.

I hope she's not as smart as I think she is, he thought.

CHAPTER 8

Dawn pulled her car into the zoo parking lot and raced up the back stairs. She zigzagged her way through darkened hallways, eventually ending up in medical records. She was rummaging through Willie's medical record a few minutes later, hastily thumbing through the two-inch thick file.

"Where the hell is it? I could have sworn it was here."

She flipped through the file a few more times before reluctantly putting his records back into the folder and sliding the file cabinet drawer closed. She sat back deep in the chair, stared at the ceiling, and thought.

∗   ∗   ∗

"Hello Michael, it's Robert."

There was a long pause on the other end of the phone before Michael Anderson responded.

"It's been a long time. Too long. It's good to hear your voice. How's your mother?" Michael's voice was hoarse and muffled.

"She's okay. Doing great actually. How about you?"

Michael coughed and cleared his throat.

"Getting older, I'm afraid. I haven't been able to shake this damn cold. I hope you're calling to tell me you've cured the common cold and can put an end to this interminable suffering."

"No, nothing like that, I'm afraid," Robert replied laughing. "But, cold or no cold, I need to speak with you in person. I was hoping you could find the time to meet with me tomorrow. It's important. Really important. You know I wouldn't ask if it weren't. You're the only one I can trust."

There was a moment of silence before Michael responded.

"Meet me here at noon."

"You got it. Thanks, Michael."

"Good, I'll see you then. Make sure to say hello to your mother for me. Will you?"

"I will. Oh, and please don't tell anyone I'm coming, Mom included. Okay?"

"Okay," Michael replied, sounding a little uncertain.

⋆   ⋆   ⋆

Dawn sat still with her eyes closed, struggling to clear her head. The more she concentrated, the less she remembered. Twenty-five minutes passed with nothing to show for it.

"This isn't working, I might as well go home and get a fresh start in the morning," she muttered, getting up and leaving the room. She passed by her office and was halfway down the last set of stairs when suddenly she stopped dead in her tracks.

"How could I be so stupid?" she said, turning and running back up the stairs. She rushed into Dr. Borelli's office, opened the file cabinet, and found what she was looking for a few seconds later. It was a file containing newspaper articles dating back to when Willie was found in East Aurora. She quickly skimmed through the news articles until she came across the passage she was looking for.

The chimp was found wearing a blue and white New York Yankee's baseball cap with the initials R. P. printed in black ink on inside rim. There was no other identifying information found.

"R. P.,…it doesn't make sense. This happened more than twenty-three years ago. What the hell's going on?" Dawn wondered.

CHAPTER 9

Michael heard the distinctive crushing sounds as Robert's car tires churned the loose gravel in his driveway. The noise of the car door slamming closed was followed by footsteps on the farmhouse porch, and several knocks on his front door.

"Come in, the door's open," Michael yelled from the bathroom. "I'll be right there. Make yourself at home."

Robert slowly opened the door, stepping out of the bright sunlight and into the dimly lit house. He paused to let his eyes adjust to the darkness. It had been nearly three years since he had last set foot in the house, and he was surprised to see how much had changed. A huge fieldstone fireplace, surrounded by recessed maple bookcases completely covered the far wall. Five massive hickory beams sectioned off the cathedral ceiling. The hardwood floors were tongue and groove yellow pine, polished to a glossy shine. Robert stepped down into the main section of the living room, a large rectangular pit bordered on three sides by a wraparound leather sofa. An antique coffee table, two Roycroft chairs with matching end tables, and a Shaker rocking chair filled the remaining space. The farmhouse walls were bare; no paintings; no photographs, nothing hung on them at all. A solitary photograph, set in a handcrafted mahogany frame, of Edward and Michael, sat atop a stone mantle.

Michael entered the room, fastening the top button on his shirt. "You look a lot like him."

"That's what Mom says," Robert replied, without taking his eyes off the photograph.

Michael wrapped his arms around him and squeezed tightly. "God! It's good to see you. How have you been?"

"It's really good to see you too. I'd wish you would come around more often."

"Can I get you something to drink? A beer, soda, juice?" Michael asked, quickly changing the subject.

"A beer would be great."

"That sounds like a good idea, I think I'll join you. I'll be back in a flash."

"Hey, the house looks great. Did you do all the remodeling yourself?"

"Every board and nail," Michael yelled from the kitchen. "It took me next to forever to finish, but it was worth it."

Robert sat down and opened his backpack, pulling out a black binder and three large manilla envelopes.

Michael handed him a beer and sat next to him on a corner of the sofa. "So, what's so important that you can't discuss it on the phone?"

"I need your help, but first you'll have to promise me that what we're about to discuss will remain in this room. At least for now."

"Are you in some kind of trouble?"

Robert shook his head and laughed. "No, it's nothing like that. I know you and my Dad worked together for a long time and he trusted you. I need your help."

Michael leaned back, folded his arms across his chest and thought before answering. "Okay, nothing leaves this room. You have my word on it."

"You can't even tell my mother. Okay?"

Michael leaned forward, resting his forearms on his thighs. "You've got yourself a deal. I promise. Now do you mind telling me what this is all about?"

"I'd ask you to sit down but since you already are…here goes. What do you think about time travel?"

Michael was quiet, he studied Robert's face to see if he was joking. He started to speak but stopped, putting the bottle of beer to his mouth and taking a long drink instead. He ran his fingers through his dark hair without taking his eyes off Robert. "Are you asking me if I think it's possible or if it should be messed with?"

Robert shrugged his shoulders. "Both I guess," he said.

Michael put his beer on the edge of the table and scratched his chin. "The analytical side of me would say it's not possible, but I have a strong suspicion you'll have something to say about that. As for whether or not I think we, meaning the human race, should get involved with it, the answer is no. But let me hear what you have to say before we go down that road."

"Fair enough," Robert said, opening up one of the manilla envelopes. "You remember Willie, don't you?"

"He's a chimp. Isn't he?"

Robert placed a single photograph on the table. "That's right. Here's a picture of him taken five days ago."

Michael pulled his reading glasses from his shirt pocket, put them on and leaned forward.

Robert pulled another photograph from the binder and placed it alongside the first. "This was taken less than two days ago."

"I assume this is a picture of Willie too," Michael said, holding the second photo between his thumb and index finger.

Robert nodded.

Michael stood up, rubbed his hand across the stubble on his chin, ran his fingers through his hair again, and looked at the photos one more time. "Jesus, he's so much older. How the hell did you do it?"

"You have the answer right there in your hands. It all starts with pho-tographs. The theory's actually quite simple. It's the application that's a bitch," Robert said, taking another drink and reaching for his black binder. "Every time you take a photograph, atoms are captured on the film. Atoms from the exact moment in time the photograph was taken. They're frozen there, sort of in suspended animation, almost fossilized in a way. It takes a certain quantitative amount of energy to capture them, to place them on the film and keep them there."

Robert stood up and paced back and forth behind the sofa. "Suppose you're able to measure the exact amount of energy used to freeze the atoms initially and reapply it to the photograph later. Theoretically, you should be able to reverse the process and free the atoms without destroying or distorting them. For every action there's an equal and opposite reaction. Sort of a different twist to Newton's theory, when you think about it."

Robert sat back down and continued. "Think about it. You're releas-ing atoms that have been frozen in time. They could have been there for hours, days, weeks, a year or a hundred years, it doesn't matter. It's all relative. Now let's take it a step further. Suppose you were able to cap-ture and amplify the atoms at the exact millisecond they're released from the photograph. Theoretically, you would create a small portal of time. A passage back to the exact moment the picture was taken. It wouldn't matter where you were physically because time isn't depend-ent on space. They're separate continuums. A time portal would exist wherever it was created. Not where the photograph happened to be taken."

Michael was speechless. He sat back and listened intently.

"The last part of the trick, and most difficult, is to make the portal large enough and keep it open long enough to allow something, or *someone* to step inside before it closes. Once the atoms are freed, that's it. They're gone. You can't get them back again and the door they've opened is closed forever."

Robert reached into another manilla envelope and pulled out a copy of the newspaper article he had copied at the library.

"It works, Michael. It really does work. Three days ago, I sent Willie back to 1960," he said, tossing the newspaper article on the coffee table. "I visited him at the zoo the day before yesterday. The second photograph I showed you was taken then. He's twenty-three years older now." He looked Michael in the eyes. "So what do you think?"

Michael took his glasses off, tucked them into his pocket and stared straight ahead. "I think I need another beer."

*   *   *

"Do you mind closing, Matt? I'm really backed up today. I've got a ton of things to do before lunch," Dawn said.

"Not at all, I'll be fine. I've just got to cauterize a few more arteries and sew him up. I'll make sure he stays sedated through the night, and I'll keep an eye on him for most of the day tomorrow. He'll never even know he's missing an appendix. He'll be fine. Fit as a fiddle!"

Dawn peeled off her latex gloves. "Good work. I'll be sure to give you a call if I ever need an appendectomy. Give him five-thousand milligrams of penicillin and check with me before returning him to his cage. He'll need something for the pain tomorrow. The last thing we need around here is a pissed off polar bear."

She was at her desk a moment later, holding Robert's business card in one hand and a phone in the other. She rehearsed opening lines in her head, dialed, and hung up a couple of times before finally mustering up enough courage to call. His answering machine picked up her call on the fourth ring.

"Hello, Robert, it's Dawn Mackey, from the zoo. I'm going to be out your way tomorrow and wanted to see if you're free for lunch. I'll be here all day, call if you can. Thanks, talk with you later." She sat back in her chair, stared out the window and thought about Willie.

*   *   *

"Can you get back to the present after you go back?" Michael asked, still half in shock.

Robert smiled nervously. "That would be the sixty-four-thousand dollar question. In theory, all you would need to do is bring a present day photograph back in time with you and apply the same technology. It should act in the same manner and open a passage back to the present day."

"But you don't have any way to test that theory. Do you?"

Robert shook his head. "No, there's no way to know without going back and trying it."

"You can't go through with it. Don't you think your mother's suffered enough? What happens if you can't get back? What happens if you're stuck back there? The only reason she survived your father's death was because she had you. She needed you more than you needed her. You can't take the chance. Too much can go wrong. Way too much! It's not worth the risk," Michael warned.

"If not me then who?" Robert yelled. "I'm the only one that knows how it all works. I can't ask someone else to do this and you know it. This is something I have to do myself." He stood and walked over to the fireplace. "I'm not looking for your seal of approval, or permission. I've already made my decision. Don't you think I've thought of all those things? I've done a ton of research on this. It's all in my journal. It'll work. I'm positive. Absolutely positive. I wouldn't have sent Willie back if I had the slightest doubt."

"And what if something goes wrong? What if it doesn't work and you can't get back? Then what?"

"Then I'll have to deal with it."

"But will your mother? How will *she* deal with it?"

Robert turned and stared coldly at Michael, trying to remain calm. "Let's not go down this road. Okay? It's been the most difficult decision I've ever had to make. I'm not doing this for the fame, the notoriety, or to win the Nobel Prize. I'm not going to try and feed you some line of crap about doing this for the betterment of mankind. The truth of the matter is that I'm doing it for me. All I want is a chance to see my father again."

Robert took the picture off the mantle and held it in front of Michael. "This is all that I have left of him," he said angrily. "Photographs and home movies. That's it! All I want is an opportunity to see him one last time. To hear his voice again. I can't tell you the number of times I've lain in bed, late at night, with my eyes closed really tight trying to remember him. Trying desperately to remember little things, like the sound of his voice, or the feel of his hand. The truth of the matter is that I can't. I can't remember anything about him," he said, pausing to wipe the tears from his face. "At least you have memories to hold onto. I've got nothing. There isn't a day that goes by that I don't think about him. Even when I go to the friggin' movies, I see a father with his son and wonder how that feels. How it feels just to sit and talk with your dad. It still hurts, Michael, even after all these years, it still really hurts. Some wounds never heal. They may look fine on the surface. But deep down, where it really matters, they never heal. So, please, I'm begging you. Can we call a truce for now?"

Michael reluctantly agreed, "fair enough," he said.

"Good. Now can we get back to work? I'd like you to have a copy of my journal. It details all of my work on this project, right up to yesterday. I have the original and plan on bringing it with me."

"Exactly what is it that you want me to do?"

"Hopefully, if all goes well, nothing."

"And if something goes wrong?"

"Then I need you to talk to my mom and take care of her for me. What do you say? Do we have a deal?"

"Yeah, I guess so. You'll go back with or without me anyway. Won't you? So, what's in the other envelope?"

"Mostly personal stuff; photographs, letters, you know, the usual things. I'd like you to give it to her if something happens to me. There's also a key for a safe deposit box. It contains a backup of the software that runs this thing, and a working replica of the hardware needed. I'll give you the passwords to the program before I leave. You can't run the program without them, and if the wrong password is entered three consecutive times, a virus is activated."

"Sort of like Mission Impossible, huh?"

"Yeah, sort of, I guess."

"When are you planning on going back?"

"Day after tomorrow. I was hoping you could be with me."

"Don't worry. I'll be there. Someone's got to keep an eye on you," Michael said, patting him on the back. "We've got a lot of ground to cover between now and then. We'd better get started. I'll need a crash course in how this thing works. I want to know everything about it."

Robert grinned, "I was hoping you'd say something like that. I just happen to have brought all of the equipment along with me. For a cup of coffee, I'll give you the nickel tour."

CHAPTER 10

Robert strolled into the Parkside Bar and Grill a few minutes before noon, happy to leave the cold and damp weather at the door. He scanned the room, before taking off his coat and sitting all alone at the bar.

"Whatta ya have?" the bartender asked.

Robert pushed his wet hair away from his face. "It doesn't matter to me. Whatever you have on draft."

"How's an ice-cold Bud grab ya?"

"It works for me."

"Do you need a menu?"

"Not right now. I'm waiting for someone. She should be here any minute now."

"I wish I had a nickel for every time I've heard that before," the bartender joked. He placed a menu on the bar. "Just in case," he said, and smiled.

Twenty-five minutes passed and Robert was still sitting by himself at the bar.

"Sure you don't want to order?"

"Let's give it another five minutes. If she doesn't show by twelve-thirty, I'll—"

The door swung open and Dawn Mackey stepped out of the cold damp air, quickly walking over to the bar. "Sorry I'm late, but it's been one hell of a morning back at the farm. I was hoping you'd still be here."

"No problem. I'm not in a hurry. I've got a pretty light afternoon ahead of me. By the way, thanks for dropping my hat off the other day."

"It was my pleasure. I really enjoyed talking with your mom. She's a terrific lady."

Robert nodded. "Yeah, she is. How about something to drink?"

"I'd love a glass of wine."

"How's Willie?" Robert asked, motioning for the bartender.

"He's fine. How's the research coming?"

"It's coming along. Slowly but surely. I really haven't had much time to work on it the last day or so."

Dawn played with her long blonde hair, nervously wrapping it around her index finger. "Speaking of Willie, I was reviewing his file the other day and came across the strangest coincidence."

"Oh, and what would that be?" Robert asked cautiously, trying not to appear too interested.

"Remember when I told you he was found abandoned in a park, a little more than twenty years ago?"

Robert glanced up and nodded slightly.

"Well, it seems he was found in Hamlin Park. Right around the corner from your mom's house."

"Really? I don't remember reading anything about that, but I would have only been seven or so at the time. I guess it's a small world after all. Isn't it?"

"Oh! There's more. It seems Willie was found wearing a Yankee's baseball cap."

Robert raised an eyebrow, feigning the appearance of surprise.

Dawn continued. "The hat had two initials on the inside rim."

I shouldn't have let him take the hat, Robert thought.

"What were they?" he asked innocently.

"R.P.," Dawn said, looking into his eyes, trying to read his reaction.

Robert smiled, "spooky, huh?" he said without hesitation. "Not only is he found near my house but he's wearing a hat with my initials. What do you suppose the odds of that are?"

Dawn didn't let up. "Your mother tells me you have a chimp named Willie. Funny how you never mentioned him to me."

"Hmm, I thought I did. Are you sure? Willie's quite a character. I've had him for close to five years now. He's like family."

"I'd like to see him sometime," Dawn said.

"Huh?"

"I'd like to see your chimp sometime soon," she repeated.

"Sure, anytime at all."

"How about tomorrow? Can I see him tomorrow?"

"Can I get you two anything to eat? The kitchen closes in thirty minutes," the bartender announced in the nick of time.

"I'm starving, how about you, Detective Mackey? Or did you stop at a doughnut shop on the way over here?"

Dawn laughed. "No. I couldn't find any that were open," she answered. "I'm sorry if I've come on too strong. I tend to be a little suspicious at times."

"A *little* suspicious! I thought you were going to break out the rubber hose and spotlight. Been reading a little too much Sherlock Holmes or what! So let me see if I've got this right. You're wondering if I had anything to do with a chimpanzee found in a park less than two blocks from my home, more than twenty years ago. A chimpanzee who happens to be wearing a NY Yankees baseball cap, with my initials written on the inside rim. And the fact that I have a chimp with the same name just adds fuel to the fire. Right?"

"It did cross my mind once or twice," she admitted with a mischievous grin.

Robert laughed. "I'll bet it was more than once or twice. Well, I don't want to disappoint you, but I didn't have a thing to do with any of it.

Maybe your chimp found one of my baseball caps in the park. I was always leaving them behind and losing 'em. It got so bad, that my Mom stopped letting me wear hats to the park. Not even old ratty ones. Some of the coincidences are just plain weird, and I can't offer any explanations. But sometimes fact is stranger than fiction. I think this is one of those times. It sure is weird though. I'll give you that."

Dawn shook her head. "Well, Dr. Paolucci, if you weren't so darn cute I wouldn't believe a single word you said."

Robert smiled. "So, what's a pretty girl like you doing at the zoo?"

"Okay, okay, you don't have to hit me over the head with a brick. Time to change the subject."

Robert grinned. "So, you think I'm cute, huh?"

CHAPTER 11

One Day Later

"Room Eight, that's my lucky number," Robert said, turning the key and opening the oversized oak door.

Michael Anderson followed him into the room, carrying a blue and white striped duffle bag. There wasn't much in the room. A large hand-crafted Roycroft dresser stood directly across from the bed, and a matching nightstand sat between the bed and balcony. The only other piece of furniture, an eighteenth century, Shaker-style armoire, stood alone against the far wall. French doors opened to a private terrace, furnished with turn-of-the-century wicker rockers and a coffee table.

Robert laid on the bed, stretched out, and put his hands behind his head. "Not too shabby, eh, Uncle Mike? This is it, Room Eight at the historic Roycroft Inn, downtown East Aurora. This is where it'll happen. I still can't believe we're doing this."

"You can't! What about me? Two days ago I was minding my own business, enjoying my retirement. All alone! Now I'm smack-dab in the middle of the craziest experiment I've ever been associated with…and your dad sure came up with some crazy ideas."

Robert draped his arm around Michael's neck and smiled. "Makes you feel young again! Don't it?"

"Among other things," Michael muttered.

"Well, let's get the ball rolling. I prepared a check list so we won't forget anything. Let's empty the bags and take an inventory. It should all be here."

Michael zipped open the duffle bag. "Sounds good to me. By the way, what date are you going back to?"

"Third week in October, 1960."

"That's just before your dad's plane crash."

"Yeah, I know."

Michael stopped unpacking and looked him in the eye. "Remember when you first asked me about time travel and I said I didn't think it was possible?"

"Sure, I remember. Why?"

"I also said I didn't think that mankind should fool around with it, but I never explained why. Well, I'd like to now, and what I'm about to say isn't intended to change your mind. I know I'd be wasting my breath. I've been doing a lot of thinking these past two days and I want you to listen carefully to what I have to say. It's important."

"Go ahead, I'm listening," Robert said, sitting upright on the edge of the bed.

Michael stood up, opened the French doors and stepped out onto the balcony. The smell from a distant fireplace slowly drifted into the room. He took off his glasses, carefully tucked them into his breast pocket and took a deep breath of the crisp country air.

"The risks are huge. The changing of a single, seemingly innocuous event could be the catalyst behind a chain reaction of events leading to catastrophic changes in the course of history. You have to be extremely careful not to change anything. The slightest change could have serious consequences. Remember, you're only a spectator back there, not a player. You have to become completely detached to all that's occurring around you. Make no mistake about it, the temptations will be great, as will the consequences associated with the decisions you make. Follow your head. Not your heart," he said, stepping back into the room and standing beside Robert.

"As tragic as it was, your father's death was an accident. I wish he'd never gotten on that plane. But the fact of the matter is that he did, and we've all had to live with the aftermath. It's not fair. Life usually isn't. But it was his time. Think before you act. You may not get a second chance. And always keep in mind the power of what you've created."

"I will. I've thought about this a long time and I know what I can and can't do. All I want is to see him again. I don't even plan on telling him who I am, not that he'd believe me anyway." Robert reached into his coat pocket and pulled out a CD-ROM disk. "I'm taking this with me. It contains all major New York Times news articles since 1960. I've loaded a copy on my hard drive so I'll be able to run a comparison of the two while I'm back there."

"What will that do?" Michael asked.

"The copy on the hard drive is protected. It won't be subject to changes resulting from time travel. The CD isn't protected. If I cause a significant change which disrupts the time continuum, I'll be able to run a comparison of the two and determine what happened. Hopefully, I'll be able to correct the problem while I'm back there. I'm bringing along a Polaroid camera and plan to take a new picture each morning just in case I need to use them to travel back in time once I'm back in the sixties."

"Are you sure you can travel back a second time?"

Robert shrugged his shoulders. "I can't see why not. Let's hope I don't need to find out." He picked up the camera and snapped a picture of Michael standing beside the armoire. "There we go. This is my ticket back. I'll use this photo to return."

*   *   *

"How are you coming along over there? Are you ready to go over the checklist?"

"Ready when you are," Michael announced.

They assembled the equipment. Ran final checks and reviewed the list one more time. Everything was in order; the dresser was pulled away from the wall, the laptop and black box were on top of it. Its opening was pointed at the wall outside the bathroom door. Two strips of masking tape, forming the letter X, were stuck to the floor approximately three feet from the wall.

"Everything looks good," Robert said as he finished measuring the distance from the aperture to the spot on the floor. He made a notation in his journal and entered the figures into the computer before putting the journal into his backpack. "Do you know what the most difficult part of this project was?" he asked, as he tied the straps of the backpack together.

"I haven't a clue," Michael answered.

"Trying to find 1960 currencies. I'm bringing five hundred dollars with me. I must have paid a thousand for it."

Michael smiled. "But think how much more you get for your money in 1960. It'll all come out in the wash."

"I don't know. I still feel as though I've been taken to the cleaners. No pun intended."

Michael laughed and put his arm on Robert's shoulder.

"How about letting an old man buy you lunch?"

"Actually, I think I owe you a lunch and a whole lot more for helping me," Robert said.

"You may have something there. Tell you what. You buy me dinner when you come back. You can tell me all about your dad."

Robert smiled. "You've got yourself a deal."

"All right then, let's get some chow. I'm starving."

*   *   *

After they returned from lunch, Robert went into the bathroom and changed. He came out a few moments later wearing a faded pair of jeans that was rolled up at the cuff, a plain white T-shirt, and a pair of black Converse sneakers.

"Well look at you," Michael said, grinning from ear-to-ear.

"All right. Let's get it over with. I know I look like a complete geek."

"Where did you get those clothes? The Salvation Army?"

"Don't laugh too hard. They were my dad's. I found them in a trunk in the attic. The jeans were a little long so I had to roll them up a few inches. The sneakers fit pretty good but they're no Nikes. Actually, I don't think I look half bad. I could only find one outfit so I'll have to do a little shopping while I'm back there."

"Boy, I hope I didn't look that bad back then," Michael said with a smile.

Robert adjusted his Yankee's cap, put his father's old wind-breaker on and threw the backpack over his shoulder. "Well, this is it. It's show time." He stepped forward onto the masking tape and flashed a thumbs-up sign. "I'm as ready as I'll ever be. Time to rock and roll."

"Any last words?" Michael asked.

"Take good care of my mom and tell her I love her."

Michael nodded. "Stay out of trouble back there. Remember what I told you. And tell your dad that he still owes me ten bucks."

"I'll be squeaky clean. Thanks for everything. See you when I see you." Robert stood up straight, swallowed his gum, and cracked a nervous smile.

Michael double clicked the mouse, stepped back, and said a prayer.

The hard drive began to hum, the red light on the black box lit up, and the CD-ROM drive made a few clicking noises. A few seconds later, the light began blinking, a high-pitched noise followed, and a brilliant reddish-orange light flooded the corner where Robert stood. The pulsating red glow encased his body and cast an oddly colored shadow on the wall behind him. He felt a strange sensation throughout his body, a tingling, electrical feeling that seemed to resonate from inside out. It felt as though every cell in his body was charged with electrical current. It was barely noticeable at first but quickly increased until his nerves fired uncontrollably and his muscles twitched rapidly. His heart rate spiked and his breathing was labored. Suddenly, his blood pressure crashed and he went numb. A brief feeling of euphoria came over him just before everything went dark.

The intensity of the light forced Michael's eyes closed. The last thing he saw was Robert's silhouette fading into the reddish-orange glow. By the time he opened his eyes again, he was gone. A peculiar burnt odor permeated the air and Michael stood motionless, wondering if he'd done the right thing.

CHAPTER 12

Wednesday, October 19, 1960

Robert was on his hands and knees, dazed and confused, wondering if he was going to throw-up. He shook his head, hoping to clear the cobwebs. "Oh Jesus, that sucked!" he groaned, struggling to his feet, talking his sunglasses off and looking around the room. Michael was gone, so were the laptop and black box. The dresser was pushed back against the wall. A thin slice of sunlight squeezed through a tiny crack between the drawn curtains in the darkened room. The odor of spent cigarettes and men's cologne permeated the stale air.

Suddenly, he realized he wasn't alone. There was someone sleeping in the bed.

I've gotta get out of here, he thought.

His eyes were still adjusting to the darkness as he quietly tiptoed toward the exit. He was less than a yard from the door when someone shouted from inside the bathroom.

"Hey, Jimmy, you better have your fat ass out of bed by the time I get out of the bathroom. We've got a ton of crap to do today."

"Eat shit," the large lump in the bed moaned. "Who died and left you boss? I'll get up when I feel like it."

Robert quickly shuffled a step and a half toward the door and reached for the knob. He quietly unlatched the security chain and slowly turned the deadbolt without making a noise. He was halfway out of the room when the bathroom door flew open, slamming hard against the wall. He quickly slid the rest of the way through the doorjamb and stepped into the hallway, closing the door behind him.

Jimmy sat up in bed. "Did you hear something, Tony?" he asked, clicking on the light and pulling a loaded 38 special from underneath his pillow. He snapped the safety off and clutched the gun tightly. His arm shook badly.

Tony stepped out of the bathroom, one towel was wrapped around his waist and another draped over his shoulder. His straight black hair was dripping wet and a cigarette butt hung from the corner of his mouth. He snatched his pistol off the dresser and cocked the hammer. "I thought I heard the door close. What about you?"

Jimmy got out of bed and cautiously walked to the door. "Me too. Did you leave the room this morning?"

"No, I got up, had a couple of smokes and took a shower. Why?"

"The door's unlocked, that's why. I know I locked it last night. I'm positive," Jimmy replied.

"Check the hallway," Tony said, sliding into his pants.

Jimmy wiped the sweat off his forehead, took a deep breath and slowly opened the door. "Nothing," he said, quickly pulling his head back after a cursory glance down the hallway.

Tony threw his cigarette butt to the floor and snapped a fresh clip into his gun. "Check and see if all the tapes are here. We'll be dead before morning if one's missing."

Jimmy fumbled through his brown satchel and counted the tapes while Tony finished getting dressed. "They're all here," he announced a moment later.

"You sure?"

"Yeah, I'm sure."

"Count 'em again."

"I counted them twice already."

"I don't give a rat's ass if you counted them a hundred fucking times. I want you to count them again. NOW!"

Jimmy glared at Tony but didn't challenge him. He opened the satchel and counted the tapes again. "Just like I said before, there's nothing missing. They're all here."

"What's that smell?"

"Don't know. Smells like a match or something," Jimmy answered.

"Doesn't smell like a match to me. Besides, I always toss 'em in the can after I light up."

Tony sniffed the air. "Were you screwing with your explosives again? I told you I'd shove 'em up your fat ass if I caught you messing with that shit in here."

"I've been sleeping. When would I have had time?"

Tony thought for a few seconds without responding. He looked Jimmy in the eyes and slowly turned away. "What the hell is that smell?"

"We'll see who gets what shoved up their ass. You'll be begging me to light the damn fuse when I'm done with you. You greasy piece of shit," Jimmy muttered to himself.

"Hurry up and get dressed," Tony ordered. He opened the French doors and walked out onto the balcony.

Who would want to get in here? he wondered.

He leaned against the railing, tucked his pistol into his pants, and finished his smoke. Robert turned onto South Grove Street and disappeared behind a row of maple trees before Tony had a chance to see him.

"Pack everything up. We're getting out of here. I got a bad feeling about this. We've been here too long anyway. I'm sick of this back-ass town," Tony said, spitting on the floor. "I can't even get a decent piece of ass out here." He stepped back into the room, flicked his cigarette butt onto the balcony, and closed the doors.

"Yeah, you're right. Let's get out of here. I'll call the boss and let him know what happened."

"HE DOESN'T NEED TO KNOW JACK-SHIT. Nothing happened here. Did it, asshole?"

Jimmy took several steps back, nodding as he retreated. "No, nothing happened."

"I'm going to check the car. You finish up in here. I'll be back in a few minutes. Don't forget to lock the door behind me," Tony said. He tucked the barrel of his gun into his black trousers and covered its handle with his shirt. "Don't open the door for anyone but me."

*   *   *

Tony Molino was a big, well-muscled sociopath with a short fuse and an explosive temper. His wealthy East Coast family had disowned him before he was old enough to vote. He walked into a liquor store in the middle of the afternoon on his nineteenth birthday and beat the owner with a bat, before stealing forty-five dollars from the register. The owner slipped into a coma and died six months later, two days before Tony was sentenced to six years in the state penitentiary. Attica prison cultivated and refined his hate, feeding and nurturing it. It was kill or be killed, rape or be raped. It was a way of life he would come to embrace. He drifted south, eventually settling in Houston two months after he was paroled, and found his niche in organized crime. His cold-blooded brutality earned him the reputation he longed for and he quickly moved up the ranks.

Jimmy Callahan couldn't have been more of an opposite. He was a forty-five-year-old loser who looked a decade older. He was short, fat, and timid, looking more the part of a used car salesman than a criminal. A deliberate southern drawl masked a genius IQ. A dishonorable discharge from the Navy, for unsubstantiated homosexual tendencies, cut short a promising career as a demolition and surveillance expert.

Three months after his discharge, Jimmy's former commanding officer—and lover, was found dead, dressed in drag, in an Eastside bathhouse. The Navy, fearing a public scandal during a sensitive time, conducted a cursory investigation and ruled the death accidental.

*   *   *

Tony carefully scanned the parking lot and side streets before rummaging through the trunk of the car. Everything appeared to be in order; rope, an automatic rifle with a telescopic site, two sawed-off shotguns, and two Navy footlockers, one filled with explosives, the other with electronics. A dozen boxes filled were with assorted munitions. Tony lit a cigarette, climbed into the front seat, turned the engine over, and pulled the black, '58 Rambler convertible to the front door of the hotel.

*   *   *

Robert glanced over his shoulder before stopping at the corner of Main and South Grove Streets.

Whew! That was close. Doesn't look as though anyone's following me, he thought.

Main Street was lined with cars, none newer than 1960. He was standing next to a tan, 1957 flatbed Chevy pickup with large white wall tires and matching chrome side mirrors. It was parked behind a fire engine red, 1959 Dodge Charger.

"I don't think we're in Kansas anymore, Toto," he whispered. "Jesus! I made it. I friggin' made it!"

He stepped off the curb onto the street, looking at the cars instead of where he was going. A car's horn blared. Its tires screeched.

"Hey take your head out of your ass and watch where you're going, you fucking idiot! You almost got yourself killed," Tony yelled as he swerved his car around Robert and sped onto Main Street.

"Get a grip, asshole," Robert muttered. He started to give him the finger but decided against it, remembering what Michael had told him.

So much for small town hospitality, he thought. I've got to get a hold of a newspaper and check the date.

He strolled down Main Street. A gentle breeze was blowing across the lake and the sunlight was slowly burning off the morning fog. Rows of maple trees lined either side of the street. Their beautiful autumn leaves formed a picturesque archway. Shops were just beginning to open for the day. The milkman was making his rounds and the dog warden was patrolling the streets in search of strays.

Frank's Auto Repair Shop was selling gasoline for 19 cents a gallon. A jet-black Studebaker with chrome rims and dual exhausts pulled into the station just as Robert walked by. The gas station attendant, a sixteen-year-old kid wearing a blue jump suit with the company logo stitched on the back, filled the tank, washed the windshield, and checked the oil while the driver sat in his car and talked with Frank. A carload of teenagers pulled in a few seconds later and blew their horn one too many times. Buddy Holly's "Peggy Sue" was blaring on their radio and Frank was clearly annoyed.

"Damn kids and their music," Frank said, shaking his head.

"Hey, some time today, Pops. Give me a buck's worth," the teenage driver yelled while combing his hair in the rearview mirror.

Frank painfully walked over to their car and pumped a dollar's worth of gas in the tank, without bothering to wash the windshield or check the oil. The driver poured a handful of change into the owner's hand and sped away before it could be counted.

Some things never change, Robert thought.

He walked into Vidler's Five and Dime Store a few minutes later. The tongue and groove oak floors softly squeaked with each step. "Excuse me, sir, but is today's Buffalo News in yet?" he asked.

"Right over there, young fella. There's a whole stack of 'em. Hot off the press, just came in a half hour ago. Help yourself."

Robert walked over, took a newspaper from the rack and handed the old man two quarters. "Thanks, have a nice day," he said on his way out the door.

"You're not from around here. Are you, son?" the old man asked.

Robert stopped and slowly turned around. "Why do you ask?" he said nervously.

"Cause the paper's only a nickel."

Robert nodded and smiled. "No, I'm not from around here. Keep the change anyway. By the way, can you tell me where the nearest diner is?"

"Village Diner's down two blocks on the left. They make one hell of an omelette, and fifty cents will cover everything, including a refill on the coffee."

"Thanks, I'll keep that in mind."

As soon as he was a few feet away from the store he stopped, opened the paper, and checked the date. "Wednesday, October 19, 1960" was typed in the upper left corner just above the weather forecast. Robert sat down on the curb, stared off in the distance and wondered what his father was doing.

A short time later, he sat in a corner booth at the Village Diner, drinking a cup of coffee and reading the newspaper. "Kennedy to Campaign in Buffalo, October 23, Election too Close to Call" the head-line read.

That's the day before Dad died, he thought.

"Would you like something to eat?" the waitress asked, pouring more coffee into his mug.

"No thanks, I'm not really hungry. I'd just like to sit here a little longer if that's all right with you."

"Sure thing, take your time, honey. Let me know if you change your mind."

"Thanks. I will," Robert said smiling.

CHAPTER 13

"I'd like a room for a few days, possibly longer," Robert said, standing alone at the front desk.

The clerk slipped her reading glasses off, letting them hang from the silver chain draped around her neck and slid the morning newspaper under the ledger. "Do you have a reservation?" she asked politely.

"No, I don't. This trip was sort of a last minute thing and I couldn't call in advance. Do you have any vacancies?"

"We're usually booked months in advance, but today must be your lucky day. An hour and a half ago I would have turned you away but a pair of businessmen in suite eight checked out unexpectedly earlier this morning. It's yours if you want it."

"Eight just happens to be my lucky number. Why don't you sign me up for the week?"

"It'll be nine-ninety-five a night and that includes the best breakfast on this side of Lake Erie."

"Great. You've got yourself a deal," Robert said, laying five ten-dollar bills on the counter and signing the ledger. "Can I ask why the two men left? Was there anything wrong?"

"They didn't say anything to me and I'm glad they left, to be perfectly honest. They gave me the creeps; out all night, not coming back 'til late in the afternoon. I swear they spent more time in that Rambler of theirs than they did in their room."

Robert looked up. "A black Rambler convertible?"

"Yes, how did you know?"

"I was almost run over by one about an hour and a half ago. The driver really lit into me, too."

"That would be Tony, he was like that," she said, nodding her head while wrapping her hair around her index finger. "He was mean as they come. His partner, Jimmy, was quiet but he scared me more than Tony. There was something odd about him, something bottled up, really deep inside. Can't see it or put a finger on it but it's there just the same. Yeah, I'm glad they're gone. Won't rent a room to either of 'em again. Least not while I'm here. I hope I never see them again."

"What type of business were they in?"

"They never said and I never asked. Do you need help with your luggage?" she asked, changing the subject.

"Nope, all I have is my backpack. I'll need to do some clothes shopping though. Any suggestions?"

"There's Marty's Men's Shop on Main and North Willow. They have just about everything you need. Marty's my cousin's husband. Tell him I sent you. He'll give you a discount."

"Thanks. I'll take a walk over there a little later."

Robert picked up the room key, stuffed the receipt into his pocket, and walked down the hall. He entered the room, tossed his newspaper and jacket on the bed, and sat down.

"I guess it's time to see Dad," he said, taking the phonebook from the nightstand and flipping through the pages. "Let's see if Mom and Dad have the same phone num—, shit, the damn page is missing. What are the odds of that?" He tossed the phonebook back into the drawer, picked up the phone and dialed. "Guess I'll try their number and see if it's still the same."

Robert went blank the moment he heard his mother answer the phone. Her first hello didn't receive a response and there was a long delay after her second. She was just about to hang up when he mustered enough courage to respond.

"Hello, my name's Dr. Finaldi. I'm a professor at Cornell and I was hoping to speak with Dr. Edward Paolucci," he said, making up the story as he went.

"My husband's at UB this morning. I'd be happy to give you his office phone number. He should be there most of the day."

"Thanks, that would be great, if it's not too much of a bother."

"It's no bother at all. I was a little concerned when you didn't answer right away. We've had quite a few hang-ups lately."

"I'm sorry to hear that. I had to clear my throat, that's why it took me so long to speak."

"No problem at all. You can reach Edward at 555-4686."

"I'll do that. Thanks again and have a nice day."

     *   *   *

Robert cautiously steered the '58 Chevy rental car into the parking lot behind the Physical Sciences building at UB. It had been years since he'd driven a car with a clutch, and even longer since he'd driven one without power steering. He managed to jerk the car into a parking spot in the corner of the lot after a few stops and starts.

Pretty nasty driving, I hope no one was watching, he thought.

"Hey, wake up!" Tony said, nudging Jimmy's shoulder. "Isn't that the punk I almost ran over this morning?"

"What's going on? Why the hell are you shaking me so damn hard?" Jimmy asked, still half asleep.

"Isn't that the guy we almost ran over this morning? Over there by the back door."

Jimmy squinted and pulled the car visor down. "It's hard to see his face from here. The goddamn sun's in my eyes."

"Give me the binoculars," Tony ordered, waving his hand in front of Jimmy's face while keeping his eyes trained on the figure entering the building. "That's the same son-of-a-bitch. I'd bet a week's pay on it."

Jimmy bent over and pulled the binoculars out from under the seat. "So what if it is? What's the big friggin' deal? Don't you think it'll look a little suspicious using these in broad daylight?"

Tony jerked the binoculars from Jimmy's chubby hand. "Just give me the binoculars before he gets to the door. Damn! Too late, the prick made it in before I could see his face. Damn it! It was him. I'm sure of it. I remember the jacket he was wearing. The professor's got one just like it."

"That's a coincidence. I wonder what the odds of running into him out here are?" Jimmy asked.

Tony tossed the binoculars in the back seat, pulled out a cigarette, and struck a match on the dashboard. "I don't believe in coincidences. He could be working for Greg Jackson for all we know." He took a long, deep drag from his cigarette and blew smoke in Jimmy's face. "Are all the bugs working?"

Jimmy held up a portable tape recorder and grinned. "Yep, every-thing's working great."

"Good. Keep it that way. I want to find out who the hell he is and what he's doing here."

"And I thought I was paranoid," Jimmy muttered. "Best keep the cof-fee away from you today."

                *   *   *

Robert walked into the dimly lit building and headed down the cor-ridor toward the Physics department. He turned into the first office with an open door. Norma Maxwell sat at her desk in the outer office and greeted him.

"Hello, may I help you?" she asked as she continued hitting the type-writer keys.

Robert recognized her face from old photographs but couldn't remember her name.

This is really weird, he thought.

"Hi, I'm looking for Professor Paolucci. Do you know where I could find him?"

"Sure, he's teaching a class in the lecture hall. Let's see now, that would be Room, two-forty-two. He had to fill in for—"

"Norma! Hold up on that report. I've got a few more changes that need to be included before it's sent to Major Adams." The rear office door flew open and Michael Anderson rushed to her desk. He held a pen in his mouth, a coffee cup in one hand, and a stack of papers in the other. He bent over and spread the papers across her desk.

Robert barely recognized him. He was so different from the easy-going retired man he had left in the hotel room just a few hours earlier. Michael was halfway through explaining the corrections before realizing someone else was in the room.

"I hope you're not here to see me, because you're not on my calendar and I've got way too much to do this afternoon," Michael said abruptly.

"Not to worry, Mr. Anderson, I'm looking for Dr. Paolucci."

Michael put his glasses on and stood up. "Have we met before?"

Robert shook his head. "No, I don't believe we have."

"Then how did you know my name?"

"I noticed the name on the office door and assumed it belonged to you."

Michael glanced over his shoulder at the door and shook his head. "I must go in and out of that door a hundred times a day and I still forget my name's etched on the glass." He took his glasses off and slid them into his shirt pocket. "I'm sorry, but I didn't catch your name."

"My name's Robert Finaldi. I'm a professor at Cornell. I'm in town visiting and thought I'd drive over here and see if I could meet with Dr.

Paolucci. I've read quite a few of his papers and wanted an opportunity to speak with him."

"He's teaching a quantum physics course this morning. Isn't he, Norma?"

"Yes, room two-forty-two," she answered.

"He's pinch hitting for us today. We have a ton of professors out with the flu. The class should end in ten minutes. You're welcome to wait here if you want," Michael offered.

"Thanks, but I think I'll go for a walk."

Michael nodded. "By the way, what do you teach at Cornell?"

"I stopped teaching a year and a half ago. I'm just doing research now. I have a medical degree and a doctorate in biophysics."

"Strange combination. What made you decide on those two fields?"

"My Dad was a physicist and my Mom's in medicine. I couldn't make up my mind so I decided to do both."

"I bet your folks are proud of you."

Robert hesitated and forced a smile. "Yeah, they are," he said quietly. "I think I'll take a walk by Dr. Paolucci's classroom and sit, in if you don't mind."

"Sure, go ahead," Michael said, turning his attention back to the papers scattered across Norma's desk.

Robert walked up the stairs and down the long hallway, stopping a few yards from Room 242. He shut his eyes and listened to the muffled voice seeping out from behind the closed door. It was a voice that hadn't filled his ears in more than two decades. A voice he thought he'd never hear again. He inched slowly toward the door, straining to hear every word. He felt tense and nauseous; his heart pounded hard against his chest. His body swelled with emotions. He stopped just outside the door, too nervous and too afraid to go further. He stood all alone, leaning against the wall and listening for a while longer, wiping away the tears. Finally, after a few long and difficult minutes, he took a deep breath and opened the door.

✶   ✶   ✶

Jimmy was restless, hungry, and bored. The three doughnuts and two cups of coffee he had downed an hour earlier weren't cutting it. "Nothings happening, let's get some lunch," he suggested.

Tony continued staring out the window, not bothering to turn his head or respond, a lit cigarette dangled from his lips.

"Come on, I'm starving. We've been here all friggin' morning. Let's go get something," Jimmy begged.

Tony took a long drag from his cigarette, inhaling as much as he could. He turned his head and blew smoke in Callahan's face again. "I want to find out who that son-of-a-bitch is and what he's doing here."

Jimmy turned away and cleared the smoke with a newspaper. "He's probably a professor or something. Besides we've got Paolucci's office and home bugged. He can't so much as fart without us knowing. Come on, let's go to get a hamburger or something, I'll buy. Whatta ya say?"

"All right, already! Quit your damn whining. I swear, you're worse than a fucking old lady," Tony complained, taking one last drag from his cigarette and flipping the butt out the window. "We'll run up to the Bailey Inn. I could go for a cold beer and an order of ribs. I want to check out that blonde waitress with the big knockers. She's been looking me over ever since we walked in the joint. That bitch is itching to get porked."

Jimmy rolled his eyes and laughed. "Have you been sucking on the tailpipe or drinking your aftershave again? I don't know what she's looking at but it sure as hell ain't you. The only thing she likes about you is the tips you leave."

Tony sneered. "You'll see, I'll nail that bitch before we're through."

*   *   *

The lecture hall was dark, except for a single beam of light cast by a slide projector. Tiny particles of dust, too small to cast a shadow on the screen, floated in and out of the bright light. Edward Paolucci casually leaned against the podium, one arm comfortably draped over its top, the other holding a long wooden pointer.

Robert slipped inside and took a seat in the back just as the carousel on the slide projector clicked for the last time.

"And that should just about do it for today. Any questions?" Edward asked the class.

No one raised a hand.

"Okay then, remember to read chapters eight through eleven. There could be a quiz in your not too distant future. Now get out of here and have a good evening."

The lecture hall erupted with conversations and the sounds of students gathering their belongings. Robert remained seated in the back of the room, struggling to keep his emotions in check. Within minutes, all of the students had left and he and his father were all alone.

"Can I help you?" Edward asked as he scooped up a pile of papers and stuffed them into his briefcase.

Robert swallowed hard, clearing the lump in his throat. He began speaking, almost stuttering at first.

"Hello. I'm Professor Finaldi from Cornell. I was told I would...umm," he cleared his throat again, "find you here. I've...a...I've read most of the articles you've published and am quite an admirer of your work." He stood up and slowly walked down the stairs.

Edward lifted the carousel from the projector and slid it into a cardboard box. "Are you in the field?"

"I guess you could say half of me is," Robert replied, feeling a little more comfortable.

His father raised an eyebrow.

"What I mean is, I have a doctorate in biophysics and a medical degree."

"My brother, Tom, graduated from Cornell Medical School a couple of years ago. Do you know him?"

Robert shook his head. "Can't say that I do, but I didn't graduate from Cornell. I've only been there for two years. All of my graduate and undergraduate work was completed at Boston College."

Edward offered his hand just as his son cleared the last stair. Robert stood face-to-face with his father, holding his hand for the first time in twenty-three years. He struggled to hold back the tears. He felt like a kid again, a little boy who desperately wanted to hug his father and tell him that he loved him.

"What brings you to Buffalo?"

"I…umm…came back to see my dad."

Edward grabbed the slide projector and tucked it away in the storage cabinet. "So you're interested in some of my work."

"Yes, I've been impressed with your work for years."

"Thanks, I'm afraid I can't take all the credit though. I have an excellent team working with me. Are you involved in something similar?" Edward asked.

"There's some crossover. Although my work's more theoretical; mostly application analysis and modeling. I'm currently working on invasive uses for lasers. But most of the real-world applications are years away."

"Sounds interesting. I bet my brother would like to talk with you. Hey, do you have some spare time?"

"Sure, I've got nothing going on the rest of the day, why?"

"Great, why don't you check out my lab. It's not state of the art, but it's sure close."

"That'd be great."

"All right then, let's do it. By the way, I like your jacket. I have one at home just like it," Edward said, turning the lights off and closing the door behind him.

Robert smiled. "Actually, it's my dad's jacket. He doesn't know I borrowed it."

CHAPTER 14

Greg Jackson was nervously pacing back and forth in the hall outside Edward's office.

"Hey, Greg, how's it going?" Edward yelled as he and Robert rounded the corner.

"Can you spare fifteen minutes?" Greg asked, looking warily at Robert.

"Sure, what's up?"

Greg glanced at Robert and back again at Edward.

"Greg Jackson, meet Dr. Robert Finaldi," Edward said.

"Pleased to meet you," Robert replied, squeezing Greg's hand firmly.

Greg gave a slight nod and forced a smile. "Likewise," he muttered before turning toward Edward. "Is there somewhere we can talk in private?"

"Sure. Will you excuse us for a few minutes?" Edward asked.

Robert took off his jacket and wrapped the sleeves around his waist. "Take your time, I've got all day."

"Let's go to the courtyard," Greg suggested.

"What's going on, Greg? You seem a bit jittery."

"I don't know for sure but I think someone's been watching me. I don't have any proof. Not yet anyway."

Edward sat on a bench alongside Greg. He leaned forward, resting his elbows on his thighs.

"What about you? Have you noticed anything strange going on lately?"

"Nothing that comes to mind right away. But I really don't pay attention to that sort of thing. Who would spy on us anyway?"

"You don't know my uncle. That son-of-a-bitch is capable of anything." Greg picked up a handful of small stones and tossed them into the flower bed. "Where did Finaldi come from?" he asked, rolling a single stone between his thumb and forefinger.

"I just met him a few minutes ago. He's a professor from Cornell. I don't think he's a spy, if that's what you're asking."

Greg shook his head. "Actually, I thought he was a cousin of yours or something. He sort of looks like you. Don't you think?"

"Hmm, I don't see the resemblance, but you know what they say about Italians…we all look alike," Edward joked.

"Yeah, among other things," Greg said laughing.

"Well, I can't blame you for being a little paranoid. You've been through a lot, especially with your uncle. It certainly can't hurt to be a little more cautious. Especially now that we're so damn close to cracking this thing wide open."

Greg put his hand on Edward's shoulder. "Be careful," he warned.

"Always am, pal."

"How's the wife and kid?"

"They're great. You should bring your family over for a barbecue before the weather changes. You don't want to get caught out my way when the snow flies. We usually get three times what the city gets."

"Sounds like a plan. Let's do it."

"I'm heading to Boston for a convention in a few days. How about when I get back?"

"I'll mention it to my wife. I know Brett will be excited. He and Robby make quite a pair. Don't they?"

"Yeah, a real dynamic duo."

Greg smiled. "Like two peas in a pod, huh?"

      *   *   *

"Hurry up and finish your food. We've got to get back," Tony demanded.

"Cool your jets, skipper. We've only been here forty-five minutes. The world's not going to come to an end. Besides, I thought you were going to score with the bimbo over there," Jimmy said, pointing to the full-chested waitress leaning against the far side of the bar. "I thought you said she was in heat. Wanted you *real* bad!"

"It's just a matter of time before I nail her, fat boy, and you better wipe that smirk off your face, before I wipe it off for you. Now get your fat ass moving. I don't give a shit whether you're done eating or not."

Jimmy gave him the finger behind his back, crammed a handful of fries into his mouth, and stood. "All right. I'm coming."

"Don't forget to pay the bill. You owe me lunch. Remember?"

Callahan pulled a ten-dollar bill from his wallet and tossed it on the table. "Yeah, yeah, I remember," he grumbled, following Molino out the door. "I can't wait to kill you. You friggin' knuckle-dragger," he whispered, thinking Tony was too far away to hear.

Tony spun sharply and grabbed Jimmy by the collar. He jammed his fat body up against the wall, lifting him off the floor. He thrust his massive forearm deep into his throat, cutting off his air. "WHAT DID YOU SAY TO ME?"

Jimmy struggled in vain, quickly exhausting the last of his oxygen. His face turned ashen and he felt faint. "I didn't say anything, honest I didn't. Please, let me go," he gasped.

Tony squeezed harder, staring at him with cold, penetrating eyes. "You better watch your mouth, fat man. Next time I'll shove my pistol in it and blow your fucking head off!" He slowly eased his forearm back.

Jimmy dropped to his knees, gasping for air.

Molino walked outside, lit a cigarette, and laughed out loud.

*   *   *

Edward walked into the center of the room, leaned against a table, and held out his hands. "Well, what do you think? Quite a lab, huh?"

Robert surveyed the room from one corner to the other. It was crammed full of laboratory equipment, books, and cabinets. There were oscilloscopes, cathode-ray guns, Bunsen burners, test tubes, and beakers. Shelves were overflowing with equipment, some of which Robert had never seen outside of old text books. It was as primitive of a lab as he'd ever laid eyes on, looking more like a display at the Smithsonian. But this was 1960. Vacuum tubes were slowly being replaced by transistors, and microprocessors wouldn't be invented for another twenty years.

"I can honestly say that I've never seen anything like it," he replied.

"It took me years to get all of this stuff, but it's been worth the wait. We're on the verge of some important breakthroughs and this new equipment is really going to help. It's a shame I'm not going to be here long enough to enjoy it though."

"Why not?"

"I've decided to go into the private sector. Remember the guy you met earlier?"

"Greg Jackson?" Robert asked.

"Yep, Greg and I are partners. I'll be working at Jackson Enterprises full-time by the first of the month."

"Do you mind if I ask why? It seems as though you really like it here."

"It's a long story. Deciding to leave was one of the most difficult decisions I've had to make. But I think it's the right one. I've got a wife and son to think about."

"How old's your son?"

"Seven, he's a great kid, and smart as a whip too. What about you? Do you have kids?" Edward asked.

"Nope. I'm still a bachelor. Footloose and fancy free as they say."

"Well, don't wait too long. Kids are great. They make it all worthwhile. Every time I come home from work and see Robby looking out the window, waiting for my car to turn into the driveway, I forget about all the problems here. As long as I have my family, there's nothing else I need." He pulled a small black and white photograph from his wallet and handed it to Robert. "Here's a picture of my wife and son," he said proudly. A broad smile covered his face.

Robert fought back the tears as he stared at the photograph. Emotions welled deep inside, threatening to explode. He started to say something but stopped and gathered himself. "You have a beautiful family. I'm sure they love you as much as you love them," he said after a long pause.

"Look at me. I don't mean to bore you with photos of my family. The next thing you know I'll be showing you home movies. I'm sorry, I know you came here to see the lab and talk about my research."

Robert shook his head and smiled softly. "No need to apologize. There's nothing boring about it, believe me. It brings back a lot of memories. Reminds me of when I was young."

"Well, sometimes I get a little carried away. If you're in town long enough maybe you can stop over and meet them."

"That would be great. I'd love to."

"Maybe you can stop over for dinner. I'll talk to Helen and see what's going on this week."

"Thanks for the invitation."

"Don't mention it. Now let me show you the rest of the lab."

*   *   *

"Hey, that's the guy from this morning. Isn't it?" Jimmy asked.

Tony snapped his head around, adjusted the binoculars, and waited for the figure to clear an evergreen tree. "Yep, that's him all right. Hurry, grab the camera and get a few pictures. I'll swing the car around and get the bastard's plate number."

Robert caught a glimpse of the black convertible jutting out from behind the corner of the building and noticed that there were two men sitting in the front seat. One had binoculars draped around his neck. "That doesn't look right. Let's see if I can get a closer look," he whispered, easing the car out and swinging it around the far side of the lot.

"Hey, he's heading this way. What are we gonna do?" Jimmy asked.

"We're going to sit here and pretend nothing's going on. You got that?" Tony replied.

"But he'll see us."

"So what! He doesn't know who we are or why we're here. Just relax and don't do anything stupid." Tony slid his hand under his jacket and unbuttoned the strap on his shoulder holster.

Robert cut a wide path around the parking lot, stopping at the edge of the building. He paused for a few seconds before pulling alongside their car.

Tony pulled his gun out, cocked the hammer and held it in his lap while Jimmy buried his face inside the morning paper.

"Excuse me, gentlemen, can you tell me how to get to the thruway?" Robert asked, peering inside their car.

Tony put a finger on the trigger of his gun and never took his eyes off Robert's hands. "Turn right onto Main Street. The thruway's down about three miles on the left. You'd have to be an idiot to miss it."

Robert smiled and waved. He caught a glimpse of the tape recorder and headphones that were partially covered in the back seat. "Thanks for the help. Have a good day, fellas."

That's him. That's the asshole that almost ran me over this morning. What are they doing here? Robert said to himself.

He turned onto Main Street and drove until he was out of sight before pulling over and writing down the Rambler's plate number.

"He knows where the thruway is," Tony said, sliding his pistol back into the holster. "I got a bad feeling about him. A *real* bad feeling."

"Why would he come up to us like that if he wasn't legit?" Jimmy asked. "Nobody's *that* stupid."

A thousand thoughts raced through Tony's head. None were good. "I'm getting sick of this job. Sick to fucking death of it! All we do is sit here with our thumbs up our ass. If it were up to me, I'd take care of things right now," he said, punching the dashboard as hard as he could. "Right fucking now!" he yelled. "How long will it take to run the bastard's plates?"

"It's almost five o'clock. The DMV will be closed in a few minutes. We're going to have to wait until morning,"

Molino took his sunglasses off and turned toward Callahan. "Check it out first thing in the morning. I want to know everything about him—his name, where he lives, who he works for, and if he stands or sits when he wipes his ass. I want to know everything!"

"Sure, first thing in the morning."

Tony lit a cigarette, started the car, and sped away. "Let's go back to the hotel for a while. Paolucci's moonlighting at Jackson Enterprises tonight. I want to listen in and see how he's progressing with that bullshit project of his. Hopefully he'll finish soon so we can take care of business and get back to Houston."

"Should we call the boss?" Jimmy asked.

"Let's find out who the asshole is first. He may want us to cap the bastard."

✦   ✦   ✦

Robert tossed his jacket on the bed, took the phone book from the nightstand, and flipped through the yellow pages. "Let's see now, which one of these private investigators is close by?"

An investigator by the name of Charles Moore, with an office on Oakwood Avenue, was the only listing in East Aurora. Robert didn't need a top notch investigator. All he needed was a license plate check on the Rambler. Any private investigator with more than a day of experience under his belt could handle such a simple request. The office was only a few blocks away so he decided to go for a walk.

*   *   *

Charlie Moore sat back in his chair, resting his feet on the corner of the desk. Half of a deck of cards sat in front of him. The other half was scattered on the floor by the waste paper basket. He picked a card off the pile on his desk, carefully positioned it between his first two fingers, and tossed it toward the basket. It spun through the air, flipped over a couple of times, and landed harmlessly on the floor—three feet from the basket. He took a long sip from a half-empty pint of Jack Daniels, grabbed another card, and tossed it toward the can. The results were the same.

"Damn, I can't buy a basket tonight, Casey," he said, reaching for the bottle again.

His black Labrador retriever lifted his head, glanced at Charlie for a moment, studied the pile of cards on the floor, and curled back up in front of the radiator.

*   *   *

Less than a decade earlier, Charlie Moore had been a county sheriff with a promising future. After only three years on the job, he was headed for a promotion to the Detective Bureau. At age 24, he would have been the youngest detective ever appointed. But a routine breaking and entering call in the dead of winter would change all that forever.

It was a brutal winter night. High winds and wet snow had cut off power to most of the village. Officer Moore was less than a half-hour away from the end of a hellish double shift when the call came in on his patrol car radio—breaking and entering at 223 Tremont Street. He was wet, cold, hungry, and exhausted, but he knew the other patrol car was too far away to respond in time. So he hit the siren and lights and punched the accelerator. What he didn't know was that the dispatcher had transposed the last two numbers of the address. As he pulled his patrol car in the driveway of the wrong home, he saw a young man lurking in the shadows by the rear door. He jumped out of his car, trained his searchlight on the back of the shadowy figure and drew his gun. The man pivoted sharply, turning toward Officer Moore. The beam of light cut through the falling snow and reflected off something in his hand. A split second later, Officer Moore's gun discharged and a young man lay dead in the freshly fallen snow. The shadowy figure turned out to be a nineteen-year-old kid who was returning home after finishing the second shift at his father's textile mill. The patrol car's search light had reflected off his key chain and a tired police officer had pulled the trigger a split second too soon. Although an Internal Affairs investigation and Grand Jury probe cleared him of any criminal responsibility, Charlie Moore couldn't forgive himself. He wallowed in self-pity and guilt, quickly spiraling into a deep depression. He found comfort in the bottom of a bottle, deciding to drown his problems with whiskey rather than deal with them. And less than two years after the shooting, he had lost his wife, his home, and his job.

∗   ∗   ∗

Casey jumped up and ran to the door, barking at the top of his lungs before Robert had a chance to knock. Charlie scrambled to pick up the cards and ditch the whiskey.

"Hi, I'm Charlie Moore. What can I do for you?" he asked, popping a mint into his mouth.

"I'm Robert Finaldi. I was hoping you'd be able to help me with a personal matter," Robert said, ignoring the stench of alcohol on his breath.

"Come in, personal matters happen to be my specialty," Charlie snickered, clearing a pile of old magazines from a chair. "Please sit down."

Casey walked over to Robert and sniffed his trousers one leg at a time before letting him pass.

"Quite a loud watchdog, isn't he?"

"His bark is worse than his bite. He's more of a companion than a watchdog. It can get pretty damn lonely in my line of work. So what type of personal matter do you need help with?"

Robert handed over a scrap of paper. "I need you to run this plate number for me."

Charlie glanced at the paper and tossed it on the desk. "Do you mind telling me why?"

"I think my wife may be cheating on me. I saw her get into a car with two men, and scribbled down their plate number."

Charlie noticed his ring finger was bare but didn't pursue it. "I'm pretty busy but I should be able to get the information to you in a few days. You'll have to pay in advance though. It's company policy."

"How much?"

"Twenty-five."

Robert placed twenty-five dollars on the desk. "I'll give you twenty-five now, and another twenty-five if you turn it around in a day."

Charlie scooped up the bills and stuffed them into his shirt pocket. "You've got yourself a deal, mister."

"Good, I'm staying at the Roycroft. You can reach me there."

    *   *   *

"It's awfully quiet in there," Jimmy said, rubbing his eyes with the palms of his hands, fighting to stay awake.

"Paolucci's alone. Did you expect him to be talking to himself?" Tony said.

Jimmy rolled his eyes and shook his head in disgust. "I'm going to the store to get something to eat," he announced. "Here, take the headphones and listen while I'm gone."

"Pick me up a cup of joe. Black, no sugar, fat man.".

"You want anything to eat?"

"What are you getting?"

"A couple of candy bars."

Molino slid the headphones over his ears. "Yeah, that sounds good. Pick me up one too. Nothing with peanuts."

"I'll be back in a few."

There wasn't much to listen to. Edward was working alone and hadn't uttered a word since he spoke with his wife on the phone, more than two hours earlier. Tony was bored and his mind wandered. He kept thinking about his encounter with Robert earlier in the day. Something was going on. He was sure of it. He didn't know what, and that bothered him. He didn't like surprises.

Jimmy returned a few minutes later with a bag full of candy bars.

"What's going on?" he asked, emptying the bag onto the front seat.

"Nothing. Dip-wad Jackson just arrived a few seconds ago," he said, looking down at the collection of junk food piled on the car seat. "Jesus Christ, Jimmy, did you clean out the whole store or what? I thought all you were getting was a couple of candy bars."

Jimmy laughed. "They had a sale. Ten for a buck. You can't go wrong. Besides, last time I bought two candy bars you ended up eating both of 'em. Here's your coffee. Give me the headphones back."

*   *   *

"How's it going?" Greg asked.

"Good, I think we're getting there, slowly but surely." Edward answered. He slid a test tube into the centrifuge. Set the speed. Turned it on and made a few notations in his log.

"It's hard to believe we're so close to having cars run on water.".

"Not just cars. Any combustible engine will run on hydrogen. All we have to do now is find a way to store it as a liquid and we're in business."

"And my uncle will be out of business," Greg said, grinning from ear-to-ear.

"Yep, there won't be much of a need for gas once we get this sucker up and running. I suppose the old man will have to find a new line of work." Edward jotted down a few more notes and slid the pencil behind his ear. "I think he'll have a hell of a time trying to sell his refineries. Won't be much of a market for them."

"I live for that day! I can't wait to see the expression on the old man's face when he learns I have the patent."

$$\star \qquad\qquad \star \qquad\qquad \star$$

Jimmy adjusted the volume on the headphones. "The stupid bastards! They don't have a clue to what's going on," he said.

"What are they talking about?"

Jimmy held up his index finger, motioning for Tony to wait. "They're on the way out," he said, slipping the headphones off and stuffing them in his jacket. He hit the stop button on the recorder, ejected the tape and turned it over to Molino.

"Any progress?" Tony asked.

"I think the professor's getting pretty damn close. It shouldn't be too much longer now." Jimmy crammed a whole candy bar in his mouth.

Tony looked at him and cringed. "What a friggin' slob."

Jimmy tried to laugh but his mouth was too full.

Molino tossed his coffee out the window, lit a cigarette and started the car. "That's the best news I've heard all week. I can't wait to get out of here. Come on, let's go back to the hotel and grab a beer. I think the Knicks are on the tube tonight. We'll catch the tip-off if we hurry."

"You better step on it. We wouldn't want to miss that! Just what I want to see. Grown men bouncing a stupid orange ball all night," Jimmy snickered. Half of the candy bar was pushed to one side of his cheek and a steady stream of brown, gooey drool slid down the corner of his mouth.

Tony looked over in disgust. "Didn't your parents teach you any fucking manners? I've seen pigs that eat better than you."

Jimmy smiled, wiped the drool away with his sleeve and gave him the finger. "So what's your point?" he muttered.

CHAPTER 15

Thursday, October 20, 1960

Robert had just returned to his room after an early morning walk when the phone rang.

"Good morning, doc, it's Charlie. How was your evening?"

"Good I guess. There's not a whole lot going on at the Roycroft this time of year."

"I imagine not. Anyway, I've got the information you wanted. Why don't you stop by in a little while?"

"Great! I'll be there in an hour. Thanks for turning it around so quickly."

"Not a problem. I knew you were anxious and my connection at the DMV just happened to get in early this morning. I'll see you in an hour."

*   *   *

Robert walked around the building to the side entrance and Charlie swung the door open before he had a chance to knock.

"Come in, doc. Can I get you a cup of coffee?"

"No thanks, had two cups already. What do you have for me?" Robert asked anxiously.

Charlie refilled his mug and sat down at his desk. "I checked the plates like you asked, and found out that the car's registered to a company by the name of Lone Star Oil. They're based in Texas but have holdings all over the U.S." He took a long sip from the mug and continued. "Oddly enough, they don't have any companies or subsidiaries in this area. Or in New York for that matter."

"What about the two men? Anything on them?"

"Not yet. But I'm working on it."

"You've done quite a bit more than a plate check."

"Well, the truth of the matter is, I'm not all that busy and I thought you'd want to know."

"I appreciate the extra effort and I'd like to purchase more of your services. If you have the time that is."

"You'll have my undivided attention. I'm a little light on clients this month. As a matter of fact, you're my only one."

Robert smiled. "I need to know everything about Lone Star Oil and the two men in the car. And I need to know it yesterday!"

"Piece of cake, doc."

"Will fifty bucks be enough to start?" Robert asked, reaching into his wallet.

"More than enough." Charlie opened a desk drawer, took out a bottle of Irish whiskey, and poured two shots into his mug. "Can I ask you something? You don't have to answer if you don't want, 'cause it really doesn't matter to me anyway. I just like to know what I'm stepping into. That's all."

"What do you want to know?" Robert asked cautiously.

"This ain't got nothing to do with your wife. Does it?"

Robert shook his head. "I'm not married," he admitted. "I'm not sure what's going on, Mr. Moore. It may be nothing at all, but I need to be sure. I'm just looking out for someone I care a great deal about. That's all there is to it."

"Are you in danger?"

"No, I don't have any enemies. Not here anyway."

"Fair enough. Just be careful, 'cause sometimes you can step into someone else's business and before you know it…you're in a world of shit. I know, 'cause I've been there."

"Thanks for the advice but I don't think anything will come of this. You can reach me at the Roycroft. Leave a message with the front desk if I'm not in."

*   *   *

Callahan hung up the phone and tore the top piece of paper off the notepad. "The car's a rental," he announced.

"From where?" Tony asked from across the room.

"Southtowns's Rental. It's a small company located in your favorite neck of the woods."

"East Aurora?" Molino grumbled

"Give the man a cigar!"

Tony finished his cigarette. Strapped his holster across his shoulder and tossed a few gun clips in his pocket. "Let's go for a ride," he said, walking out the door.

*   *   *

"There it is, over there on your left, ya see it?" Jimmy asked.

"I could see a hell of a lot better if you'd get your fat hand out of my face," Tony complained. He pulled the car into the gravel driveway, tossed a cigarette butt out the window, and snapped open the strap on his shoulder holster.

"What are you planning to do with that? We're here to ask a few questions, not to kill anyone." Jimmy twisted the rearview mirror toward his face, ran a comb through what little hair he had, and adjusted his tie. "Ah, perfect. Do you know why I can't wait until tomorrow…'cause I get better looking every day! Let me handle this. Just sit back and watch a pro. You might just learn something. Anyone can pull out a heater and threaten the piss out of 'em, but it takes real talent to con 'em. You need quite a bit of sophistication to pull it off. Something, I'm sorry to say, you're sorely lacking." He opened the door and continued talking. "Two bucks says the owner's a hayseed with a mouthful of missing teeth who never got past the sixth grade. It'll be like taking candy from a baby."

"You've got your head way too far up your ass. Go ahead and ask all the questions you want. You've got ten minutes to find out who rented the car. After the ten minutes are up, we do it my way," Tony sneered.

"It'll take me less than five minutes, but I'll take ten if you're giving it. Loser buys lunch."

"You're on, fat boy!"

Jimmy walked into the rental office, rang the silver bell on the counter and waited. Tony sat on a couch in the waiting room, flipping through an old magazine, and keeping as much of his face covered as possible. Linda Whalen set aside October's invoices and left the back room to answer the bell. Her husband, John, was working on a transmission in the rear garage.

"Hello, may I help you?" Linda asked, gently pushing her long black hair away from her deep brown eyes.

"Good morning, miss. How are you today?" Jimmy asked.

"Just fine, and you?"

"Couldn't be better. My colleague and I were hoping to rent a car from you today. We'd only need it for two days. Isn't that about right, Tony?"

There was a long pause before Molino responded. "Yeah, sure. That sounds about right," he mumbled from behind the magazine.

"You're in luck. We happen to have a car available. It's our last one. I'd be glad to show it to you."

"That would be fantastic. Wouldn't it, Tony?"

"Yeah, why don't you go take a look. I'll be out after I finish this article."

Tony waited for them to turn the corner before jumping up and looking behind the counter. He quickly searched the counter top and drawers for files or receipts, but didn't find any. "Where would that bitch keep the damn receipts?" he whispered.

Frustrated, he turned and walked to the back room just as John Whalen was sliding out from under the car he'd been working on for the past two hours. Tony flipped on the lights and scanned the room. He was too far away to hear Jimmy's whiny voice but knew he'd only have a minute or two before they'd be back.

The back room was cluttered with old tables, file cabinets, auto parts, and tools. Stacks of invoices sat on top of one table, canceled checks and receipts on another.

John Whalen finished scrubbing the grime from his hands and headed out the door. His head was buried in a copy of 'Sports Illustrated' as he made his way up the brick walkway leading to the office.

What a mess. I'll never find anything here. I should have done this my way, Tony thought. He grabbed a handful of invoices, looking for Robert's plate number. He never heard John Whalen open the side door and walk into the front office. "Where is it?" he whispered as he sifted through a second stack of invoices. "Come on, give me a br—got it," he said, stuffing the yellow invoice deep into his pocket.

"Hey, Linda, are you back there?" John Whalen asked.

Tony reached under his jacket and eased his pistol out of its holster, snapping off the safety at the same time. He squeezed himself between two file cabinets, screwed a silencer onto the end of the gun, and waited.

The doorknob turned, Tony crouched down further, his knees dug sharply into his chest. He pointed the pistol at the door and cocked the hammer. John Whalen opened the door and stepped into the back room. Tony slid his finger over the trigger, took a deep breath and waited.

*   *   *

"I'm sorry to put you through all this trouble but we're looking for a car with more trunk room," Jimmy said.

"Don't mention it. It was no trouble at all. That's what we're here— wait a minute! I just thought of something. My husband's been working on a station wagon. It's in the garage. You're more than welcome to it if he's done with it."

"You don't have to go to—."

"Hey, John! Can you come out here?" Linda Whalen shouted.

Her husband took a few steps back and turned his head. "I thought you were in the back room," he yelled.

"No, I'm out here in the lot with a customer. Come out here for a minute. Will you?"

He tossed the magazine on one of the tables. Turned off the light and stepped back into the office.

Tony wiped the sweat from his brow and exhaled. "Jesus Christ! That was close." He put his gun away, slowly opened the door, and eased his way back into the waiting room without being seen.

He held the voucher to the window when neither of the owners were looking and motioned for Jimmy to wrap it up. A couple of minutes later they were driving north on Seneca Street, heading back to their hotel.

"Man, am I good! I could have kept her talking all day. I told you I can bullshit with the best of 'em," Jimmy gloated. "She was starting to tell me about her two friggin' grandchildren just as you held the paper up to the glass. She would have told me her life story if I'd let her. What a dumb-ass bitch."

"Don't ever use my real name again," Tony snarled. "Do it again and I'll kill you."

Jimmy laughed. "Relax, man. Take it easy. They're just a couple of hayseeds. A grease monkey and a grease monkey's wife. That's all. They probably spend most of their spare time reading the Farmers Almanac, for Christ's sake. That is if they can read at all. Cool your jets. Will ya? Why don't you have a smoke or something? You're way too uptight."

Molino swerved off the road and slammed on the brakes, sending Jimmy's face crashing hard into the dashboard, opening a two-inch gash above his eye. He had his gun out before Jimmy's head recoiled a second time. Tony grabbed him by the back of the neck and shoved the barrel of his gun deep into his mouth, chipping his front teeth and tearing into his gums. A stream of blood poured from his head and mouth, running down his chin and dripping onto his shirt. Jimmy gagged on the cold steel and warm blood. His heart jumped and stomach sank. Sweat rolled off his forehead into his eyes. Searing pain swirled through his body but he was too afraid to utter a sound.

"You little puke! I'm gonna blow your goddamn head off right fucking now!" Tony spit in his face, slid the safety off and cocked the hammer. He squeezed his fat neck, cutting off most of his air. Jimmy's body trembled, veins in his neck and face bulged, and warm urine ran down his leg. He was helpless, all he could do was close his eyes and pray. For a few anxious seconds, even Tony wasn't sure if he was going to pull the trigger. But he didn't. Instead, he eased up on the hammer, slowly backed the gun out of Jimmy's battered mouth and let go of his neck.

"I'll pull the trigger next time," he said, leaving little room for doubt.

Callahan didn't say a word. He didn't look up. He didn't move. He watched Tony wipe blood off the barrel of his gun and slip it back into its holster. They drove a few miles before Jimmy mustered enough nerve to raise his hand and wipe the blood from his face. Neither man said another word for the remainder of the way to the hotel. But Tony would glance over at Jimmy every so often and laugh.

Chapter 16

Robert closed the menu and slid it to the edge of the table. "Thanks for coming," he said.

A full-figured waitress, wearing a low-cut top and leaning forward in the most revealing manner possible, scooped up the menus, took their order, and retreated to the kitchen. Robert stared. Edward pretended not to notice.

"I'm glad you called because I wanted to invite you over for dinner tomorrow night. My wife's already picked up the steaks so you better say yes," Edward said, and smiled.

"I'd love to come over. I've got nothing planned."

"Great, how's six?"

"Sounds good to me. I'll be there. Can I bring anything?"

"Nope. Not a thing. Just yourself."

Robert smiled. *A bottle of wine couldn't hurt,* he thought. He poured milk into his coffee, slowly stirring it with a spoon. "I've been thinking about your storage problems with liquid hydrogen and I have a few suggestions on how you might get around some of the roadblocks."

"I've been trying to solve that problem for a while now and I'm getting nowhere fast. I'd appreciate any advice you have."

*   *   *

Tony sat in the couch and looked over the invoice he had stolen earlier. Jimmy was in the bathroom tending to his wounds.

"Robert Finaldi, huh? It says he's a professor at Cornell. Also says he's staying at the Roycroft." He lit a cigarette and tossed the spent match into a glass ashtray.

An ant walked across the table in front of him, clutching a bread crumb in its mouth. Tony let it get close to the edge before guiding it back to the center of the table with the heat from his cigarette. He watched the tiny ant scurry away, still clutching the crumb. He played with it a little longer, nudging it with his cigarette every time it got close to the edge. Each time the ant would turn and run, still holding onto the tiny crumb. Finally, after a few minutes, he let the ant clear the table's edge and walk down the leg to the floor. He watched it for a few seconds, letting it think it had escaped before slowly crushing it with the heel of his boot. He smiled, took a long, slow drag from his cigarette, leaned back in the sofa, and watched a ring of smoke float up to the ceiling.

"I say we check Finaldi out. See if he's the real deal," Tony said.

Jimmy didn't reply. He was busy trying to close the cut above his eye with butterfly bandages. He knew he should have gone to the hospital but didn't want to give Molino the satisfaction.

"When you're done playing with yourself in there, I want you to make a few phone calls and find out all you can about this guy. The invoice is on the coffee table. I'm gonna grab some chow. I'll be back in a while."

Jimmy remained silent.

Tony put his coat on and walked to the bathroom door. "You got that, asshole!"

"Yeah, I got it," Jimmy muttered.

       *   *   *

The desk clerk caught sight of Robert before he rounded the corner on the way to his room. "Dr. Finaldi, I have a message for you," she yelled from across the room.

Robert walked back to the desk and was handed a note.

Doc,

I got the information you were looking for. Call me ASAP. It's important!

Charlie

*   *   *

"Are you sure about that, Lew?" Jimmy asked, squeezing the phone between his shoulder and jaw while scribbling on the back of the invoice.

"Yeah I'm sure. I'm telling you that there's no Dr. Finaldi at Cornell. He doesn't exist. Are you sure it was Cornell? Cortland isn't too far from Cornell. Maybe he teaches there."

"It says Cornell on the invoice but check out Cortland anyway."

"That's gonna take some time. I probably won't have anything for you until late tomorrow."

"It's gotta be by tomorrow. No later. Okay?"

"You'll have it tomorrow. Even if it means putting Johnny on it."

"Good, you know where to reach me. I'll talk to you later."

Callahan hung up the phone, folded the invoice, and shoved it in his shirt pocket. "Maybe Tony was right," he said.

*   *   *

Robert placed a twenty on Charlie's desk and sat down. "What do you have for me?"

Charlie Moore slid the twenty into a drawer, pulled out a yellow notepad, and leaned back in his chair.

"It seems Lone Star Oil is owned by a gentleman from Houston by the name of Daniel Jackson. He's worth a ton of scratch, has holdings throughout the states. All in the oil business. My source in Houston tells me he's a gem. A real piece of shit. Lone Star used to be owned jointly by Daniel and his brother, Jeb, until an explosion on an offshore rig a few years back."

Charlie opened the file drawer. Hauled out a bottle of whiskey and topped off his coffee. "Sure I can't interest you in a little bit of Kentucky's finest?"

"No thanks," Robert said, holding out his hand.

Charlie shook his head and smiled. "You don't know what you're missing, doc. Now let's see, where was I?"

"You were telling me about the explosion."

"Oh yeah, the explosion. That's right. It seems that the Jackson brothers were the only two people on the rig that night. Pretty convenient, huh? They never did find his brother's body. A lot of folks think it's tied to a chunk of steel on the bottom of the ocean."

"What about the police? Wasn't there an investigation?" Robert asked.

They found a few irregularities in Jackson's story but nothing substantial enough to send it to a Grand Jury. They didn't have much of a case without a body anyhow. Besides, the old bastard owns half of Houston and—"

"Is he related to Greg Jackson?" Robert interrupted.

"I was just getting to that. I take it you know him?"

"Not exactly. He's more of an acquaintance."

Charlie picked up his coffee mug and leaned back in his chair, studying his client for a moment. He knew Robert wasn't telling him everything.

"Greg Jackson was Jeb's only child. There was a hell of a fight between him and his uncle for control of the company. To make a long story short, the old man kicked the kid's ass in court and sent Greg and his family packing. He's one ruthless son-of-a-bitch, that's for sure. Needless to say, there's some real bad blood between the two. I think it's safe to say they won't be exchanging Christmas presents anytime soon."

"What about the two men in the black convertible? Got anything on them?"

Charlie wiped his mouth with his sleeve. "Believe it or not, what I've just told you is the good news," he said, sliding his notes across the desk. "Here, take a look at this."

Robert read while Charlie talked.

"I did a little snooping around town and was able to come up with their names. I ran a check to see if anything came up. I bet a good ninety-eight percent of the checks I run come up clean. Once in a while, I'll turn up a juvenile record or some minor bullshit; resisting arrest, petit larceny, drunk and disorderly. Shit like that. But not this time. Not with these fellas. They definitely represent the other two percent. Tony Molino and Jimmy Callahan. Two real life bad guys."

Charlie finished the last of the coffee and cleared his throat. "Molino's a former New York City hoodlum with a rap sheet as long as your arm. He's done time for murder, armed robbery and rape. He's also been linked to a ton of shit that he's never been convicted for. He's been on Lone Star Oil's payroll for almost two years now. They've got him listed as a security consultant. He's got one nasty reputation. You'd be wise to stay as far away from him as possible.

Callahan's another piece of work. His rap sheet's a whole lot shorter but pretty colorful nonetheless. A few incidents of indecent exposure. A dishonorable discharge from the military. Nothing in the same league as Molino but not the type of guy you want hanging around the wife and kids just the same. He has a military background in electronic surveillance and explosives, and guess what? He's on the books at Lone

Star...as a security consultant. Now either Lone Star does a piss poor job of screening applicants or they're pretty tight with the mob. You're a smart guy. What do you think?"

Robert studied Charlie's notes for a moment before getting up and walking to the window.

"These are bad people, doc. Really bad people. How do you fit into this?"

Robert forced a small opening in the blinds with his fingers and peered out at the parking lot. "I don't and that's the truth. But a friend might. I honestly don't know what's going on, Charlie."

"I'd have a good long talk with *your* friend and find out just what the hell's going on if I were you."

"Find out what you can about Greg Jackson. I need to know if he's involved somehow."

"I'm already working on it and should have something for you in a day or two. Don't worry, I'll get you the skinny."

Robert turned, opened the door and stepped into the hallway. "Thanks, you know where to find me."

"Take care of yourself and keep your back to the wall, if you know what I mean." Charlie's voice echoed in the landing as Robert walked out into the cool autumn night. A stiff breeze swirled in the air and an uneasiness settled in around him. Streetlights cast eerie shadows across the sidewalks, spilling out onto the road. He took the long way back to his hotel. He glanced over his shoulder every so often, wondering if Molino and Callahan were out there, sitting in their black Rambler, watching and waiting. He walked briskly, staying mostly on side streets and out of the shadows.

Friday

"I'm telling you. You're chasing a ghost, Jimmy. There's no such person. Finaldi doesn't exist anywhere," Lew said for the third time.

Jimmy's eye was nearly swollen shut. A deep, purple bruise ran from his eyebrow to the top of his cheek bone. A cut above his eye, held closed by butterfly bandages, was crusted over with dried blood. And the throbbing headache that had kept him awake most of the night continued its assault on his skull.

"He ain't a ghost. I can tell you that much. He's flesh and blood all right. I need to find out who he is and what he's doing here. Keep looking, Lew, and call the second you find something. Anything at all."

"You'll be the first to know. Hey, you and Tony should lay low for a while. Someone's been asking a lot of questions about Lone Star and the two of you."

"Who?"

"We don't know yet. Tommy's looking into it. Jackson's really pissed off. He wants to speak to you and Molino later today. You're supposed to call back at two-thirty. Got that?"

Jimmy's headache got worse. "Yeah I got it. We'll call back later."

"Make sure you're on time and it's a clean line."

"What's going on? What did Lew say?" Tony asked, stepping out of the bathroom and zipping up his pants.

"There's no record of Finaldi at Cornell, or anywhere else for that matter. Bottom line is that we don't know who the asshole is or what he's doing here."

Tony tucked his shirt into his pants. "I told you something was up with that guy. I had a bad feeling about him the second I saw him. I say we pay him a visit and—"

"There's more," Jimmy interrupted. "We've got trouble. Seems as though someone's been asking a lot of questions about us."

"Finaldi?" Tony asked.

"Don't know for sure yet. Tommy G's on it. The boss wants us to lay low until they get more information. We're supposed to call him this afternoon." Jimmy grabbed a bottle of aspirin off the counter, dumped a handful into his mouth and washed them down with a can of orange soda.

"Lay low?" Tony screamed. "We should grab that son-of-a-bitch and put the squeeze on him. We'll find out what he's up to and who he's working for. Lay fucking low! What good is that going to do?"

Molino was on edge and the last thing Jimmy wanted to do was set him off. So he sat down on the sofa, a safe distance away, and didn't open his mouth. He just listened to Tony vent and waited for the aspirin to kick in.

*   *   *

Tony pulled the car alongside a payphone and waited until 2:30 before sliding a nickel into the slot and dialing. A gruff voice answered before the phone rang a second time.

"Yeah."

"It's me, Tony."

"Is Jimmy with you?"

"Yeah, he's here."

"Is the line clean?"

"Yeah, it's a payphone in the middle of nowhere."

There was a long pause. Tony could hear muffled voices in the background.

"What's going on?" Jimmy asked impatiently.

Tony ignored him, trying instead to pick up as much of the muted conversation as he could.

"How close is Paolucci to completing the project?" Daniel Jackson barked into the phone. He voice was hard and flat.

"Seems to be pretty close. Could be any day now."

"I hear you've run into a little trouble."

"Nothing I can't handle."

There was another long pause, only this time Tony couldn't hear anything.

Jackson spoke again a half a minute later. "Tell me how you'd handle this *little* problem?"

"I'd have a conversation with Finaldi. Man-to-man. He'd be spilling his guts within fifteen minutes. Maybe less. I've done this hundreds of times. Never had a problem with any of 'em. They all talked sooner or later. Mostly sooner." Tony's voice was flat and emotionless.

"Do you know if he's the asshole who's been sticking his nose in my business?" Jackson asked.

"Haven't heard for sure yet. Tommy G's working it. But I bet it's him. I'd bet my house on it. I didn't like him from the moment I saw his fucking face. Let me have him for a few minutes and I'll find out who the bastard is and what he's up to."

"And what happens if you're wrong and he's not involved?"

"I'll cap his ass anyway. Don't worry, there won't be any loose ends. I'll dump the bastard's body in a place where it'll never be found. It'll be a clean hit. Spic and Span clean."

"We don't need to bring attention to ourselves. Not when we're this close. Be patient. You'll have your chance. I want you and Jimmy to wait for now, no contact with Finaldi until Tommy reports back. I need to know if my nephew's involved. You and Callahan back off until we know for sure. Am I clear?"

"Yeah, we'll lay back until we hear from Tommy."

"You lay back until you hear from me!" Don't fuck this up, Tony. We're too close to getting Paolucci's research. I don't give a damn about Finaldi. He's yours once I give the OK."

Molino hung up the phone and turned toward Jimmy.

"We have to sit with our thumbs up our ass until Jackson hears from Tommy."

Jimmy nodded, folded a newspaper under his arm, and opened the car door. "How long before Tommy gets in touch with us?" he asked.

"Supposed to be later tonight. He's working on it now." Tony got in the car, slammed the door closed and drove back to the hotel.

           *   *   *

Robert drove around the block a few times before he was convinced he wasn't being followed. He pulled the car into his parents' driveway and sat with the engine idling for a short while.

"Dinner at Mom and Dad's. And they say you can never go back home again."

He took a deep breath, pulled the keys from the ignition, and headed up the steps.

The storm door swung open, narrowly missing his forehead, before he had a chance to reach for the doorbell. A skinny seven-year-old boy wearing a baggy white T-shirt, jeans, and black Converse sneakers stood directly in front of him. A New York Yankee's baseball cap hid most of his short brown hair.

"Are you the guy that's coming over for dinner?"

Robert stood and stared, not saying a word. He stared at the seven-year-old boy who stood before him. He stared at himself.

This is weird, he thought. *Way too weird.*

"And you must be Robert. I've heard a lot about you."

"I've got a baseball mitt autographed by Mickey Mantle. You want to see it, mister?"

Robert knelt down on one knee and smiled. "You bet I would. Mickey just happens to be my favorite Yankee."

"Hey, he's my favorite too."

"Well, what do you know? How's that for a coincidence?"

"Good evening, glad you could make it," Edward said, walking into the foyer. "I see our doorman has already greeted you."

Robert nodded. "Yep, he was just about to show me his baseball mitt. Rumor is that it's a Mickey Mantle original."

Edward smiled. "He loves that glove. Takes it everywhere he goes. He even sleeps with it."

"I use to do the same thing when I was his age," Robert said smiling.

"Come on, mister, let's go. It's in my bedroom."

"Why don't you go get it and bring it to Dr. Finaldi?" Edward suggested. "I'd like your mom to meet him."

The little boy thought about it for a split second before turning and running down the hall toward his bedroom. "Don't move, mister. I'll be right back," he yelled anxiously.

"He seems like a great kid," Robert said, feeling a little uncomfortable about giving himself a compliment.

"He sure is. Wouldn't trade him for anything."

Robert handed his father a bottle of wine. "Here, this is for you and your wife. I hope you like it. I also took the liberty of buying your son a small gift. It's a G.I. Joe set. I'd like to give it to him, if it's all right with you and your wife."

"That's right up his alley. You couldn't have picked a better gift. He's always playing with that stuff."

"I had a hunch he'd like it."

Helen walked into the room and stood alongside her husband. Robert couldn't get over how young she looked. All of the pictures he had of his father were when he was a young man, still in his thirties. So he looked exactly as he had expected. But until this moment, he hadn't realized just how much his mother had aged over the years.

"Perfect timing, honey. We were just about to come looking for you. I'd like you to meet Professor Finaldi from Cornell," Edward said. "Professor Finaldi, this is my wife, Helen. My better half."

Robert enjoyed the evening with his parents and as time wore on, the oddity of the situation faded. He was finally home again and everything was right in his life for the first time since his father climbed aboard Flight 687 to Boston. His emotions ran deep. He wondered whether he'd have the strength and courage to let his father climb aboard the plane. He wondered if he could stand to lose him a second time.

*   *   *

Jimmy slammed the phone down. "Grab your coat. We've got a name and address." He quickly slipped his jacket on, zipped open his leather satchel, checked the contents, and walked briskly into the hallway.

Tony grabbed his coat, swung his holstered gun over his shoulder, and followed. "What's the deal? What's the prick's name?" he yelled, slamming the door closed behind him.

"A private dick by the name of Charlie Moore. And get this, the asshole lives in East Aurora. Jackson wants us to pay him a visit. Talk with him a bit."

"It's about fucking time he started to see things my way," Tony said. "Give me the keys. I'm driving."

The sun had set a half an hour earlier and the red glow on the horizon was slowly melting into the night as Molino pulled the car up to the curb, a block and a half away from Charlie Moore's office. A few seconds later, he and Jimmy were walking along the edge of the sidewalk, being careful to stay in the shadows. They turned away from a passing car's headlights as they crossed the street and walked up the driveway. A single light shown through Charlie's windows. His run-down Chevy wagon sat alone in the gravel parking lot. His office sign swung freely with each passing gust of wind and the wooden stairs squeaked loudly under the weight of the two men. Tony crouched down at the side of the door, slid his hand under his trench coat, and clutched the handle of his revolver. Jimmy stood at the end of the landing and kept an eye on the parking lot. Three huge evergreen trees shielded the rear porch from the street, providing the perfect cover.

"I can't see anything through these curtains. What do you think?" Tony asked.

"I say we go in. Pick the damn lock before someone sees us," Jimmy whispered.

Tony eased the door open and slowly entered the room, clutching a pistol in one hand and flashlight in the other. Jimmy followed a safe distance behind. Molino inched his way through the outer office, checking behind doors and cabinets. Callahan made his way to Charlie's desk and began rummaging through his papers as his partner prowled the back room.

"He's not here," Tony reported a few minutes later. "You got anything?"

"Nothing but old newspapers, losing horse racing tickets, and a shitload of unpaid bills. Is this guy a loser or what!"

"Keep looking. There's a file cabinet in the back room. I'm gonna check it out. Make sure you stay away from the windows."

*   *   *

Casey picked up the fresh sent of a raccoon and took off with his nose to the ground, barreling through the thick underbrush. Charlie wasn't in a hurry so he decided to let him follow the scent for a while longer. He figured they'd be able to cut through a small field and come up on the southeast side of his office. There was a narrow dirt path that wound its way along a shallow pond on the outskirts of the Hadley farm just a few hundred yards ahead. It eventually spilled into a vacant field adjacent to his parking lot and squeezed its way between a fence and a row of hedges just behind his rear window. Charlie was familiar with the path. He used it when his rent was overdue and he needed to slip past the landlord.

Halfway down the path, Charlie knelt down and was just about to unhook Casey's leash when he saw the shadow of a man cross in front of his window. "Looks like we got company, Casey." Twenty minutes later he saw a second shadow.

"They're not burglars. They'd be long gone by now if they were. They must be looking for something. It's gotta be Molino and Callahan." Charlie zipped up his jacket, turned up the collar, and sat down in the tall grass. He pulled Casey close beside him, trying to stay warm. "Let's get comfortable, boy. Looks like we may have a long night ahead of us." He pulled out a flask, took a swig of whiskey and leaned back against a tree. "I sure hope Finaldi's been watching his back."

*   *   *

"How much longer you want to wait? Moore could be out all night working on a case, or at a bar drinking," Jimmy complained.

Tony was sitting in a darkened corner opposite the door. He leaned forward into the light to check his watch. "Another hour. He'll be back by then. He left the lights on. The stupid bastard can't afford the electric bill as it is. He wouldn't leave the lights on. Not all night." He leaned back into the shadows. "Stop your whining. He'll be back soon enough."

Jimmy disagreed but kept his opinion to himself. He leaned back in the chair, put his feet up on the desk and fell asleep. Tony remained out of sight in the dark. The glow from an occasional cigarette cast his intimidating silhouette on the wall.

CHAPTER 17

Saturday

Casey stood guard over Charlie Moore's shivering body, waiting patiently for him to wake. Morning light had broken over the horizon ten minutes earlier and the sun's rays were beginning to filter through the thick clouds. A cool, damp autumn breeze wove its way through the evergreen trees and tall grass, and eventually to the back of Charlie's bare neck. Casey pressed his cold wet nose into the private investigator's cheek, nudging him a few times before finally drawing a response.

"Jesus, Casey, it's friggin' cold. I can't believe we slept out here all night. You shouldn't have let me doze off like that," Charlie complained. He yawned, stretched, stumbled to his feet, and brushed the dirt from his clothes. "Let's go find out if those two assholes are still there."

He shortened his dog's leash and started down the winding dirt path, quickly coming up to the gap in the fence that gave way to the row of hedges on the southeast edge of his property.

"So far, so good. Now comes the hard part," Charlie whispered, winding Casey's leash around a weathered fence post. "You stay put and keep quiet." He loaded his revolver and silently made his way toward the rear of the building. There was only a few feet between the building and the hedges, barely enough room to walk. Branches scraped against his face and body as he squeezed his way along the narrow path. He wove his way through the litter scattered along the trail, being careful not to make a sound. His heart raced, his stomach burned, and his body trembled. It had been a long time since he'd been so scared. Longer than he could remember.

Charlie paused, wiped the cold sweat from his face, and took a drink before making his way across the back of the building. He stopped under the far window. He looked over his shoulder, cracked the window open and listened before slowly sliding it up as far as it would go. He stepped up on a rusty milk crate, poked his head through the lace curtains, and slid his lanky body through the tight opening.

What have you gotten yourself into? he thought as he slithered down the wall.

Charlie used his long arms to ease himself down to the floor without making a sound. He took off his shoes, crawled to the door and inched it opened. Cold sweat ran from his forehead to his neck. His heart raced and breath quickened. His mouth was so dry that he couldn't muster enough spit to swallow. He slowly entered the room with his pistol leading the way, nervous eyes darting everywhere. He looked behind the two doors and file cabinets and under the desk before checking the bathroom.

Only one more place left to hide, he thought, inching toward the front hall closet. His shirt, wet with sweat, clung to his trembling body. He crouched down to the left of the door, cocked the hammer on his revolver and reached for the doorknob. He yanked the door open in one sudden, forceful movement, sending it crashing hard against the wall. Plaster flew, crumbling to pieces as it hit the floor. A broom handle lurched forward and crashed into Charlie's outstretched arm, causing his gun to discharge. The bullet tore through the lath and plaster, ripping a six-inch hole in the closet wall.

"Son-of-a-bitch!" he screamed, falling back against the wall and sliding down to the floor. He wiped the sweat from his forehead with one hand and reached for his flask with the other. "No one's here. Thank God!" he muttered. Whiskey had never felt so soothing.

He sat on the floor and caught his breath. He wondered what would have happened if Molino and Callahan had still been there. He knew he had to warn Robert as soon as possible. He hoped it wasn't too late.

*   *   *

Edward rolled down the window of his car, blew the horn, and waited for Helen to come to the door.

"Don't forget that I'm working late tonight. I'm going to Jackson Enterprises right after work. I'll call you later to let you know when I'll be home," he said.

"Try not to make it too late. Okay?"

He smiled, rolled up the window, and pulled the car out of the driveway. His son stood in the living room window, watching until the car turned the corner and disappeared onto Walnut Street.

"Come on. Let's get you ready for school. That outfit you're wearing doesn't come close to matching. Did your father dress you this morning?"

Robert smiled but didn't say anything.

"I thought so," his mother said. "Honestly, it frightens me to think he has a Ph.D. and still can't match a pair of pants with a shirt."

*   *   *

Charlie let the phone ring a dozen times before giving up.

"Damn it. Where the hell could he be?" he said, pushing down the coin return and retrieving his nickel from the slot.

"Looks like we're going to have to swing by the Roycroft and check on him, Casey. I've got a bad feeling about this. A real bad feeling."

*   *   *

The Buffalo Zoo's massive black iron gates swung open promptly at 9:00 A.M. Robert rushed through the turnstile, paying the 50-cent admission fee. An old man, carrying buckets of feed, passed in front of him as he entered the main compound.

"Excuse me, sir, but can you please tell me where the primates are housed?" Robert asked.

The old man laid the heavy buckets of feed on the ground. "Monkeys are straight ahead, past the big cats. They're in a feisty mood this morning." His voice was coarse and thick with a Scottish accent. He lifted an arm and pointed toward the north end of the zoo. His blue jump suit was tattered and badly soiled. A large red rag, covered in grease, hung from his back pocket. A scraggly, gray beard covered most of his weathered face and his long hair was shoved up under a faded red baseball cap. "Don't know what's gotten into them. Musta been a full moon or something last night. They're straight away, mate. Just over the hill. I'm sort of partial to the big cats myself. They'll be feeding soon. You sure as hell don't want to miss that. What do you want with the monkeys anyhow? All they do is scream and throw shit at people all day long."

Robert smiled and walked away.

He'd fit right in at a Grateful Dead concert, he thought.

He came to the cat habitat a couple of minutes later and stopped for a moment to watch a veterinarian tend to an injured tiger cub. Its very anxious mother paced back and forth in an adjoining cage; growling and hissing loudly. A pretty blonde-haired girl knelt down beside the crippled animal and watched her father bandage its broken paw.

"Hey, Dr. Mackey, your wife called. She wanted me to remind you to drop Dawn off at the dance studio after work tonight," an attendant yelled from across the compound.

Dr. James Mackey raised an arm and responded with a short wave.

Dawn frowned and shook her head. "Can't I skip dance and stay here with you, Daddy?" she pleaded emphatically.

"How about that? It really is a small world after all," Robert said to himself, continuing on toward the chimps.

He could hear the chimpanzees as he approached the crest of a steep hill just outside the primate quarters, and the old man was right. They were loud. "I wonder what's gotten into them this morning?"

As he cleared the crest, he could see the top of a huge steel cage that rose 30 feet into the air. Willie was perched on the top branch of a white maple, clutching a ratty stuffed animal in one hand, fending off a half dozen chimps with the other, keeping it just out of their reach.

Robert laughed out loud. "Atta boy, Willie."

He stayed out of sight and watched for a while before stepping out of the shadows and walking up to the side of the cage. Suddenly, Willie dropped the stuffed animal and swung his way down the tree until he was face to face with him. "Hey, boy. It's good to see you," Robert said, reaching through the bars and holding Willie tightly. Tears ran down his face. "I really miss you," he whispered softly. Willie kissed him on the cheek, reached through the bars, and swiped the baseball cap off his head.

"You did that to me the last time I saw you. Remember?"

Willie slid the cap onto his head, smiled broadly and held out his long arms.

"I can't take you back with me, fella. I wish I could. But I can't." The tears came more quickly. He took a long, deep breath and swallowed hard. "This is your home now. It's where you belong. You'll be happy here. You've got lots of friends and they'll take good care of you. I promise. I came to say goodbye. I've gotten what I came back for and it's time for me to go home. To go back to where I belong." He reached through the bars and hugged the chimp again. "I've got to go now, Willie. You take care of yourself. Okay? I'll see you in twenty years," he said, wiping the tears away. "Have a great life. I'll never forget you. Never. I promise."

Robert held him one last time before turning and walking away. Willie stood and watched until he disappeared beyond the far side of the hill. He climbed to his favorite perch atop the maple tree and sat by himself for the rest of the morning. He left the stuffed animal for the other chimps.

Saturday Evening

"That's it! That's what we've been waiting for. Paolucci just completed the last phase of the project and the damn thing works. That son-of-a-bitch did it! We can get the hell out of this shit-hole and go home," Jimmy yelled. He took off his headphones and tossed them in the back seat of the car.

A groggy Tony rubbed the sleep from his eyes. "What's happening? What the hell did I miss?" he mumbled.

"Listen to this." Jimmy pressed the tape recorder's rewind button and clicked on play a half-minute later. Edward Paolucci's voice crackled on the tiny speaker.

"Hey Greg, it's me. Sorry to call so late but, we did it! We really did! We can cool hydrogen to a liquid and hold it for as long as we want. In other words, we're in business, partner!"

"Yeeeeeeee Haaw!" Greg yelled in his usual slow southern drawl. "Where the hell are you?"

"At the lab."

"Stay put. I'll be there in two shakes of a lamb's tail."

"Sorry, but I can't. I've got to get home. Helen's going to kick my ass, I haven't been home yet and I have a nine-forty-five flight to Boston tomorrow night. How about if I close up here and call you in the morning? There are a few minor details that need to be worked out, but nothing too difficult. Just some fine tuning, that's all. I'll be able to work on them in Boston and we should be ready to roll when I get back. Let's plan on meeting Tuesday morning here at the lab. Okay?"

"How about if I take you to the airport? We'll stop for a cup of coffee or something. That way we can talk before you leave. I'll pick you up at eight-thirty. Okay?"

"Sure, if you're buying," Edward joked.

"Don't worry I'll pick up the tab. I'll even throw in a doughnut. We're really going to be able to do it! Aren't we?"

"You bet. Nothing can stop us now."

"Hey, you better get home to Helen before she kills you."

"I know. I'm just about outta here. I'll call you in the morning."

"Good enough, I'll talk with you—oh! One more thing."

"Yeah."

"Thanks. Thanks for everything, Edward."

"Hey, I couldn't have done it without you. Now get some sleep and I'll call you in the morning."

"Talk with you then," Greg said.

Jimmy pressed the stop button.

"Excellent. Now all we have to do is grab his notes and we've got everything we came for," Molino said. "Let's get on the horn to the boss. He wanted to be here for this." He slid the keys into the ignition and turned the engine over.

"Wait! Why not get the notes, take care of the professor, and have it wrapped up before we call?"

"I don't know. He said to call as soon as the professor finished. I don't want to piss him off. You know how he gets when things go wrong," Tony responded.

"Nothing's going to go wrong. We'll say we didn't find out until tomorrow night. Right before Paolucci goes to the airport. We'll tell him that we didn't have time to call. He'll never know. Besides, he'll be so happy that we've got the research that he won't give a rat's ass about when we called. Trust me. He'll be happier than a pig-in-shit. Come on. What do you say? Let's show him we can handle matters by ourselves. Show him we're not a couple of losers who don't know their ass from their elbow. You know what will happen if we call, don't you? He'll send in a bunch of his flunkies to handle everything. We'll be tossed aside and they'll take all the credit. We've been on this case too fucking long to let that happen."

Tony gave it some thought before reluctantly agreeing to the plan.

"Good deal, partner. You won't be sorry. We'll take care of Paolucci tomorrow night at the airport. All we have to do is grab his notes before he boards the plane. I'll make sure his plane drops from the sky like a rock. Greg Jackson will figure the notes went down with the plane. The FAA will never find out what caused the plane's engines to blow. It'll explode into a million pieces. Yes sir, it'll all be over this time tomorrow and we'll be back in Houston before you can shake a stick. Trust me, Tony, I've been waiting a long time for this opportunity. Paolucci's a dead man, all right."

Molino was guardedly optimistic. As much as he hated to admit it, Jimmy made a lot of sense. "Okay, we'll get it done tomorrow night. You take care of the plane while I get his notes. No screw-ups, all right?"

"Piece of cake," Jimmy grinned. "Piece of fucking cake. All I need is a few minutes with the plane. Let's get back to the hotel so I can work on the device tonight. It'll take me three or four hours to finish. I'll drive out to the airport in the morning for a little reconnaissance work."

Chapter 18

Sunday Evening

Robert Paolucci walked onto the balcony and looked out over the south side of Hamlin Park. The time machine lay on a corner of the bed, fully assembled and ready to go. It was a quiet autumn evening. Brightly colored leaves fell from rows of maple trees and drifted slowly to the ground. A cool dry wind blew across the open grass and swirled around the tall evergreen trees that lined the far end of the park, carrying with it the soothing scent of a distant fireplace. Robert stood and stared for a long while, taking it all in one last time. He closed his eyes tightly and for the first time in a very long time, he could see his father's face and hear his voice. He finally had his own memories to hold on to. Vivid memories. Real memories. Memories to last a lifetime. A smile filled his face and the penetrating sadness that had tortured his soul for more than twenty-three years was gone. He'd gotten more than he could have hoped for and knew it was time to leave. He was ready to go back to the future. He was ready to go back home.

And then the phone rang.

"Hello."

"Is that you, doc?"

"Who's this?"

"It's me…Charlie. I've been trying to get hold of you for a day and a half. Christ, I thought they got you."

"Who got me? What the hell are you talking about?"

"Molino and Callahan. Those bastards broke into my office the other night and rifled my files. When I couldn't get hold of you I figured they had. God, I'm glad you're all right, kid."

"I haven't seen them in a few days. Not since I talked with you," Robert answered. "Why would they be interested in your files?"

"My guess is they're looking to find out as much about you as they can. They must know that I'm working for you."

"Do you know where they are now?" Robert asked anxiously.

"I was just at the airport, picking up a package for a client, and I saw their car parked there. I stayed and watched it as long as I could but I didn't see any sign of the pricks."

"What would they be doing at the airport?"

"Don't know. Maybe they're picking someone up."

"Something's wrong. Something's really wrong. I can feel it in my bones. I've got to run, Charlie. There's something I have to do."

"I'll go with you," Charlie offered.

"Thanks, but this is something I've got to do myself."

"These are bad people, doc. The kind you don't fuck with. You don't get second chances with them. You won't stand a chance going in alone."

"There's a lot you don't know and you wouldn't believe me if I told you. Thanks for the offer but I've got to go it alone. At least for now."

"I'll stick by the phone in case you change your mind. Be careful out there, will you?"

"You can count on it."

*   *   *

Robert slammed the car into park, grabbed his backpack, and raced into the east terminal. He arrived at the gate just as Greg Jackson was saying goodbye to his father. He waited until Jackson was out of sight before approaching his father from behind.

"What am I doing here?" he muttered. His steps were slow and measured. The knot in his stomach tightened. He could feel his heart pounding against his chest. He knew the smart thing to do would be to turn around and walk away, to go back home. Back to the future. Back to where he belonged. But he couldn't bring himself to do it. He couldn't turn back. Not without knowing the truth.

Suddenly, a large, dark figure stepped out of the shadows, crashing into him, knocking him off balance.

"Hey, watch where the hell you're go—" Robert jerked his head sharply to the left just in time to see Molino reach into his coat and draw his gun.

"Keep your mouth shut and step back behind the counter." Tony's voice was cold and harsh, and left no room for compromise.

Charlie was right. I shouldn't have come here alone. What the hell have I stepped into? Robert thought.

He slowly stepped back, retreating a foot at a time while keeping an eye on the gun.

"That's it, asshole, keep moving back," Tony sneered. His hulking frame filled the walkway. "You've been a thorn in my side since the first day I saw you. But not for too much longer."

Robert stopped just short of the counter and slowly raised his hands in the air. "You're making a big mistake. You must have mistaken me for someone else."

"Not a chance. You're the one I want."

"What do you want from me?"

Tony thrust the gun deep into Robert's side. Its barrel pressed hard against his ribs, taking his breath away. Molino leaned forward and whispered in his ear. His breath reeked of stale cigarettes. "Let me tell you how this works, pal." He pushed harder on the gun. "The guy with the gun, and that would be me, gets to ask all the fucking questions. Is that clear?"

"Yeah, perfectly clear," Robert answered, taking half of a step backwards. The airport security guard that stood at a small newsstand less than fifteen yards away was too busy hitting on a stewardess to notice what was happening.

"Good, now step behind the counter and open the door behind you. We're going to take a little walk."

"Where are we going?" Robert asked, hoping to buy a little more time. Hoping someone would see the gun.

"What did I just tell you? I ask the questions. Now shut up and move."

Robert ran out of room. He had nowhere to go. He glanced over Tony's shoulder and caught a last glimpse of his father before stepping behind the counter and reaching for the door.

Suddenly, out of nowhere, a small horde of reporters rushed into the area a few yards in front of Molino. Flash bulbs exploded everywhere, reporters jammed their microphones into the center of the crowd and blurted out questions.

Tony nervously slid his gun back under his coat while reaching for Robert's arm.

Robert saw his chance and took it. He pushed Molino aside, stepped out into the path of the oncoming mob and was swept away. He looked over his shoulder. Tony's icy stare sent shivers down his spine.

And surprisingly, through the crowd of reporters, amid the glare of flashbulbs, a familiar face emerged.

"Jesus Christ, it's JFK. I can't believe it," Robert said as Senator Kennedy walked past him.

   *   *   *

"I'm sorry that Senator Kennedy's private jet has experienced a mechanical problem and I understand that he needs to get back to Boston tonight, but unfortunately all of the seats on the nine-forty-five flight are taken. There's another plane leaving at eleven and we still have seats available," the frustrated ticket agent explained to the senator's aide for the third time. "As I've said before, I'd be more than happy to put the senator on stand-by and book a seat for him on the later flight if that's all right with you."

The aide reluctantly nodded as his candidate politicked behind him.

Robert felt a hand on his shoulder and immediately pulled away, almost stumbling to the floor.

"Hey, take it easy, it's only me," Edward said. "What are you doing here?"

Robert grabbed his father by the arm and dragged him to a corner of the gate. "I need to talk with you. It's important."

"I'll be boarding my plane in a few minutes, so we don't have a whole lot of time."

"Less than you know. You can't get on that plane. You have to come with me."

"What are you talking about? I have a seminar in Boston tomorrow morning that I have to attend. I'm presenting a paper."

Robert was frantic. "The plane will never make it to Boston. It will crash somewhere over the Appalachians. There won't be any survivors."

"What are you telling me? That you know what's going to happen? That you can predict the future? Do you expect me to believe that? What's wrong with you? Are you crazy?" Edward pulled away and stepped back toward the walkway.

Robert slid his backpack off and placed it on the chair beside him. He stepped forward, looked his father in the eye and took a deep breath. "No, that's not what I'm trying to say. I can't predict the future. No one can. I know what happens because your future is my past."

Edward was quickly becoming agitated. "What's that supposed to mean? What the hell are you talking about?"

"There's no easy way to say this to you and I doubt you'll believe me anyway." He sat down, buried his face in his hands for a moment and started talking. He struggled to find the right words at first but gradually they came to him. "I've lied to you. I'm not Robert Finaldi. There is no Robert Finaldi. It's a name I made up."

"I don't understand. Why would you lie to me? What possible reason could you have?"

Robert stood. "I may have lied to you in the past, but what I'm about to tell you now is the truth. I swear to God it is," he said, his voice was beginning to break. "Please let me finish with what I have to say before you interrupt me or walk away. You can leave if you want to when I'm done. I won't try to stop you. You have my word."

May we have your attention? All passengers on the nine-forty-five flight to Boston may now board through gate number eight. Please have you tickets ready, the airport intercom system announced.

"I don't have time for this. I've got to go." Edward picked up his briefcase and headed for the gate. Robert lunged at him, grabbing him by the arm.

"My real name is Robert Paolucci. I'm your son."

Edward stopped, spun sharply and ripped Robert's hands from his arm. "You're fucking crazy! Get out of my way. I've got a plane to catch," he demanded.

Robert grabbed his father by the arm again, squeezing tightly. "I'm not crazy. I'm telling you the truth. I've come back in time to see you. I know it's hard for you to believe. Impossible to believe, but what I'm telling you is the truth." He rolled up his sleeve and held his arm in front of his father's face. "Here, look. Look at the scar on my wrist. I got it at Sinking Ponds when I was six. You told me to stay away from the rocks but I didn't listen. It took eight stitches to close. You and Mom were with me at the hospital. Remember?"

Edward examined the scar and sat down, letting his briefcase fall to the floor between his feet. "That scar doesn't prove anything. It could be just a coincidence," he said, sounding a little less sure of himself.

"I know about the dream you had the night your brother died in Korea. You and Uncle Robert were lying under the bed and he was screaming and begging you not to let them take him away. You never told anyone about that dream, except Mom. There's no way for me to know that unless she told me." He sat down next to his father and continued. "She even told me about the ten-dollar bill you dropped on the ground and pretended to find the first night you met. Here, look at my driver's license. Look at the pictures in my wallet. They're pictures of you and her. Even if you don't believe me, you can still make it to Boston. You can take the later flight. That's all I'm asking you to do."

Edward looked back at the gate. Robert continued.

"I grew up most of my life without you, that's why I came back. I wanted one more chance to see you again. One more chance to hear your voice. To talk with you. I wanted to know what it was like to have a father." Robert cleared his throat and wiped the tears from his face. "You can't imagine how much I've missed you. I didn't come here looking to make up for all of the things I've missed over the years. I know that can never happen. All I wanted was a chance to see you and get to know you a little so that I would have something to hold onto. Something to remember. You've got to believe me. I'm telling you the truth. I won't let you get on the plane. I can't. I won't lose you all over again!"

Edward handed the wallet back and remained in his seat as the last call for the flight was announced. He leaned forward in the chair, resting his elbows on his knees. "And your mother…how is she?" he asked softly.

"Lonely, she never remarried. She still keeps your picture on the nightstand by her bed. Like me, she never got over losing you.

Sometimes I'll find her sitting on the glider in the backyard, late at night, curled up in a blanket. She'll sit there for hours. Slowly gliding back and forth, looking up at the stars and talking to you."

Edward pushed his sleeve up and glanced at his watch. He stood and stared at the gate, watching the last few passengers climb onto the plane. "How did you travel back?" he asked.

"It's a long story. I've got all the equipment here in by backpack and I'll show you once we get out of here. It's not safe here. Some people have been following you. They work for Daniel Jackson, Greg's uncle. I think they're after your research at Jackson Enterprises. I ran into one of them here when I first arrived but he disappeared. Come on. We've got to get out of here before he comes back."

CHAPTER 19

The full moon was barely visible through the heavy cloud cover, offering no appreciable illumination in the airport parking lot. Robert and his father were about to get into their car when Tony stepped out of the shadows.

"Did you miss your flight, professor?" he asked, thrusting his pistol deep into Edward's side. Jimmy pulled the black convertible up a few seconds later and Tony forced them into the back seat.

"I've seen you before. You ran into me in the hallway in my office building. Didn't you?" Edward said to Jimmy.

"Give the douche bag a cigar!" Callahan snickered.

"What's going on? What do you want?"

Molino pointed the gun at Edward's face and cocked the hammer. "Shut up and give me the briefcase!" he said forcefully, snatching it from his hand. He popped it open, pulled out the black three-ring binder, and quickly thumbed through the pages. "Is this everything on the hydrogen experiment?"

"Yeah, it's all there. Everything's in the binder. You've got what you want so now let us go."

"Do I really look that stupid? Sure we'll let you both go if you promise not tell the police. Where have I heard that one before?" Tony asked sarcastically. He pushed the barrel of the gun under Edward's nose and laughed. "Did you really expect me to say something like that?"

Just then the flight to Boston took off and roared overhead.

"Take a good look at that plane, gentlemen, because there won't be much of it left soon," Jimmy said proudly. "They'll be scrapping pieces of it off treetops in another hour or so. Man, I wish I could see it blow. Although I must say that I'm a tad bit disappointed that you're not on it, professor."

"You planted a bomb on the plane?" Robert asked.

"Please, give me a little more credit than that. A bomb makes it sound so simple. So archaic. I prefer to think of it as a highly advanced incineration device. I've utilized the most recent advances in mercury switches and chemical reagents. The last switch is tripped after the plane hits a cruising altitude of 10,000 feet for thirty minutes or so. Give or take a few seconds. Sort of a slow burn, you might say." Jimmy glanced over his shoulder and grinned. "The most challenging part was to make sure it wouldn't be detected during an FAA investigation. And that's the beauty of it. All of the components are routinely found in your standard airplane engine or are by-products of a combustion fire. In any event, they wouldn't cause an investigator to take a second look. Quite an ingenious device, if I do say so myself. The dumb bastards will think the engine caught fire and exploded. They'll probably blame it on a ruptured fuel line."

"But I'm not on the plane anymore and you've got what you want. Why blow it up?" Edward asked.

"Do you know how much time I spent working on that device? I was up most of the night. I'm not about to let all that work go to waste."

"But there are innocent people on board. Some are women and children," Edward pleaded.

"So what! There are too many people in this fucking country anyway. A couple of dozen won't be missed," Tony said.

Jimmy laughed. "I couldn't have said it better, partner."

Molino stuck a cigarette in between his lips and lit it. "Enough about the fucking plane. Let's get to the river."

"Is that where you're going to kill us?" Robert asked.

"I could pop you right here if you want, you little weasel. You've caused me nothing but grief. I don't know who you are and I really don't care anymore. You'll both be dead in a few minutes anyway."

"So where is the big man? I thought Daniel Jackson would want to be here for the grand finale," Robert said.

"We can handle things ourselves. We don't need our hands held," Jimmy snapped back.

"Shut up and drive!" Tony yelled, pounding the dashboard with his fist.

Robert worked a small knife from his pocket and closed his hand around it without anyone noticing. Jimmy took the Seneca Street off-ramp and drove for another ten minutes before pulling the car behind an abandoned food processing warehouse on the edge of the Niagara River. The rusted railroad tracks that crisscrossed behind the dilapidated building were littered with debris. It had been a decade since a train had been down the tracks, and even longer since anyone worked there. Even the rats had abandoned the building soon after the last of the rotted food had been eaten.

Tony stuck the barrel of the gun under Robert's chin and grinned. "Everybody out," he ordered.

Robert didn't move. "Go ahead, pull the trigger. Get it over with," he dared.

Tony smiled and slowly pulled the gun away. He grabbed him by the collar and pulled him out of the car. "Soon enough, tough guy. Now get in the warehouse."

Edward leaned against his son. "Don't push him," he whispered.

"They're going to kill us anyway. They've got what they want. We're just a couple of loose ends, that's a—"

Tony's fist crashed hard into Robert's face, sending him sprawling to the ground. He drew his pistol, cocked the hammer, and pulled the trigger in one fluid motion.

Edward lunged, hitting Tony's arm just as the gun discharged. The bullet grazed Robert's shoulder before ricocheting off the pitted concrete floor. Tony grabbed Edward's throat with one hand and kept the pistol trained on Robert with the other. "I told you to keep your big mouth shut. Now stand up and get inside," he ordered, slowly releasing his grip on his throat and shoving him through the door. Robert struggled to his feet, clutching his wounded shoulder. Blood had already begun to soak through his jacket.

Jimmy unloaded the trunk while Tony tied the two men to wooden chairs. He pulled the rope tight, cutting sharply into Robert's wrist.

"I'm awfully sorry if the rope's too tight. I hope it doesn't hurt too much," Tony quipped. His long, guttural laugh echoed off the warehouse walls. Callahan was crouched down in the far corner with his back to the door.

Tony fished the rope through the leg of the chair, made a knot, and pulled it tight. "Well that should just about do it. I don't think either of you will be going anywhere. Now let's take a closer look at your notes, professor. I want to make sure it's all here." He snatched the thick black binder from the table and quickly thumbed through the pages. "You know, doc, if you're lying to me and it's not all here, I'll have to pay that sweet little wife of yours a visit to see if you kept a spare copy at home. And while I'm there, I might just see how sweet she really is. Yeah, she's got one hell of an ass on her. Bet it's as tight as it looks." He smiled and winked. "If you know what I mean."

"Leave her alone! Everything you need is there. I swear to it!" Edward begged.

Robert opened the pocketknife and began sawing through the rope.

Tony leaned forward, coming within an inch of Edward's face. "I certainly hope so, for your wife's sake. If not, I'll crush her fucking skull. Right after I stick it to the whore. While your candy-ass son watches. I may even let Jimmy have sloppy seconds."

"I told you it's all there. Leave her alone. She's got nothing to do with this."

Molino reached into his jacket and slipped on a pair of black leather gloves. Robert had cut through the first of three ropes and was a quarter of the way through the second.

"As for you," Tony said, turning toward Robert. "Just who the hell are you? And what are you doing here?"

"I'm Robert Finaldi from–."

Tony buried his fist in Robert's face before he had a chance to finish.

"Do I look that stupid? We've checked with Cornell, asshole. There's no record of a Professor Finaldi on their faculty…or anywhere else. So let me ask you again and I expect a better answer this time. He grabbed Robert by the back of the hair, pulled his head back and shoved the barrel of his gun under his nose. "Now, let me try this one more time! Who are you and what are you doing here?"

Blood trickled from the corner of Robert's mouth and slowly ran down his neck. He spit a mouthful of it onto the floor and glared at Tony.

"You're awful brave while I'm sitting here tied to a chair. Aren't you? Why don't you cut me loose and show me how tough you really are, or are you afraid I'll kick the shit out of you in front of your fat-ass friend? Come on. Take a chance. Untie me, asshole. Let's see if you're half as tough as you think you are."

Tony gently slapped the side of Robert's face and smiled. He laid his pistol on the table and pulled his black leather gloves tight to his hands. "You've got balls. I'll give you that much," he said, pulling a switch blade from his vest pocket and slowly walking behind the chair. His slow deliberate steps echoed from the rafters. "There was a time when I had something to prove. When I would have taken your challenge personally," he said, slowly dragging the blade of the knife along Robert's cheek and down toward his neck. He let the blood that was dripping from Robert's mouth collect on the edge of the shiny blade.

"I spent six years at Attica proving how tough I was. And believe me. It's personal there. Extremely personal! The guards were worse than the niggers. They all thought they were tougher than me too." He brought the knife to his mouth and licked the blood off the blade. "They were wrong. Every last one of them. So you see, I've got nothing to prove. Not to a piece-of-shit like you. Not to Jackson. Not to anyone."

Tony walked back in front of the chair and held the knife a quarter of an inch from his captive's eye. "I could cut you up right now if I wanted to." He drew the knife back and thrust it deep into the post, missing Robert's face by a fraction of an inch. "But I'd get a lot more pleasure from beating the piss out of you. I've been waiting to do this for a long time."

The first blow caught Robert in the stomach, just below the ribs, and bent him in half. An uppercut to the chin sent his head crashing into the post. Tony landed a few more body shots before pausing to admire his work. Robert grimaced in pain and gasped for air. His jaw felt like it was broken, the back of his head was throbbing, and he was still bleeding from his shoulder and mouth. The rope was cutting off blood flow to his hands and his fingertips were starting to go numb. He desperately struggled to hold onto the pocketknife.

Jimmy turned his head and glanced over his shoulder. "Hey! You're not using my good leather gloves, are you? They cost me more than twenty bucks. I'll never get the blood stains out."

"Relax, tightwad, they're mine. Yours are too small," Tony yelled. He turned back toward Robert and tugged on his gloves again. "Now let's see, where was I?"

"Stop it! You're going to kill him," Edward pleaded.

"Shut your mouth or I'll kick your ass too," Molino scoffed. He grabbed Robert by the collar and pulled him close. "I'm prepared to stay here all night and play this game. It's up to you. Why did you hire that dip-shit private investigator and who are you working for?"

Robert caught his breath, spit more blood onto the floor and continued working on the ropes. "So, how many times did you get fucked in the ass while you were in prison? Bet you were someone's bitch. Weren't you?"

Tony stared with cold, penetrating eyes. He hesitated for a moment before stepping back and spitting in his face. "Hey Jimmy, we've got ourselves a *real* tough guy here. Yeah, a real tough son-of-a-bitch. Okay, tough guy, we'll do it the hard way." He pulled the switchblade from the post and pushed the point into Robert's cheek until it drew blood. He dragged the edge of the knife around his face to the back of an ear, dug it into his skin and pulled forward. Robert closed his eyes and waited. He could feel the cold steel cutting into his flesh and blood running down the back of his neck.

"Have you ever seen just how stupid people look without ears?" Tony asked. "I remember cutting the ears off this Jew lawyer in San Francisco a few years back. He had the biggest friggin' ears I've ever seen. I had a hell of a time stuffing them into his mouth before I slit his throat." He laughed and pulled on the knife some more. "Goddamn Jews, the only thing worse than a Jew lawyer is a Jew banker. Normally, I don't give much thought to killing someone. It's not all that different than stepping on a spider or ant. You do it without thinking about it. It's nothing personal. It's business. But every now and again, you run into some asshole that you just can't wait to bleed. He was one of those assholes. Just like you. Yeah, he thought he was a tough guy too. Come to think of it, he never did tell me what I wanted to know. But that's okay…'cause I gave him an earful! Hey, Jimmy, how do you think he'd look without ears?"

"It would be an improvement. Course it will be a bitch when he wants to wear sunglasses," Callahan snickered. "Hey, Tony, check his backpack before you cut him. See what's in there."

Molino laid the knife down and placed the green backpack on the table in front of the two men. "Well, now, let's see what the weasel brought with him," he said, loosening the draw sting and spilling the contents onto the table. "Holy shit! What the hell is all this crap? Hey Jimmy, look at this shit, will you?"

Jimmy walked over to the table and picked up the laptop. "Jesus! I've never seen anything like it before, not even in the military. What is it?"

Robert thought quickly. "It's a graphic equalizer. I use it to calibrate different wavelengths of sound. I'm sure you've worked with one before," he said as he continued sawing on the ropes.

Callahan hadn't a clue to what he was talking about but nodded anyway. "How do I turn it on?" he asked.

"You can't. Not without the nine-volt adapter and it's back in my hotel room." He finished cutting through the second rope. He had lost all feeling in his fingers and his muscles ached badly.

Come on. A few more minutes. That's all I need, he thought.

Jimmy picked up the black box. "What's this used for?"

"It attaches to the equalizer. It sorts wavelengths by types and then rearranges them into various patterns so that I can analyze the differences in their frequency and pitch."

Jimmy examined the laptop and black box for a moment and studied Robert's face. "I think you're full of shit. I don't know what they are or what they do but I'll figure it out later. I'm a smart guy too. Smarter than you think."

"I don't care what it does. Are you finished yet?" Molino interrupted.

"I'll be done in a few seconds." Jimmy laid the laptop down, went back to the corner, and returned a few minutes later carrying a small wooden box. "We're set," he said, offering the box to his partner.

Tony stepped back. "Don't give that thing to me. I don't want any part of it."

Jimmy shook his head and laughed. "Relax. It's harmless until I activate it. And even then we've got a couple of minutes before it blows."

"Just set the damn thing, fat-ass, and let's get out of here."

"First put everything in the backpack. I bet it's worth a lot of dough. We can sell it later. Where are the professor's notes?"

"I've got them right here," Tony said, lifting the notebook over his head. "So is that thing set? Are we on the clock?" he asked nervously.

Robert finished cutting through the last piece of rope and slipped his hands free without being seen.

What do I do now? Should I rush Tony and go for his gun, or should I wait? he thought.

He tried to calculate how long it would take to cover the ten feet between him and the gun and how long it would take Tony to react. He knew the odds weren't good, but he also knew they wouldn't get any better. He leaned forward, placing his weight on the balls of his feet and waited for Tony to look away. He hoped Jimmy was as slow as he looked and that he didn't have a gun.

If I can take Tony out quickly, I have a chance, he thought.

Jimmy carefully lay the wooden box down on the floor and walked to the door.

Robert had his chance. Tony's head was down and his gun sat on the table next to the laptop.

It's now or never, he thought.

"Hey, is it set or not?" Tony asked impatiently.

Jimmy didn't respond.

"Are you deaf? Is the fucking timer running?"

"Hey, Tony, catch!" Jimmy said.

"Catch what?" Tony asked, turning back toward Callahan.

The first bullet caught Molino in the middle of the stomach and sent him crashing backwards into the table, knocking the pistol and laptop to the floor. The second tore a hole in his upper chest, severing an artery and driving him hard to the floor. Tony would lose consciousness in less than a minute and bleed to death in a few more. Still, he managed to get to his knees one last time.

"You bastard. You fat, fucking bastard. I'm going to kill you," he yelled, lunging for his weapon.

Jimmy kicked it away and watched as he crumpled harmlessly to the ground. Deep red blood surged from his chest and spilled out onto the floor.

"I've earned this," Jimmy said, picking the notebook up off the floor. "I've fucking earned it," he repeated. "Did you think I was going to let you turn it over to Jackson so he could make a fortune and then turn around and toss me a few crumbs? Do you think I put up with all of this shit just to be another one of his lackeys?" He stood over Tony's dying body and went off. "Did you think I would forget about everything you put me through or forget what you did to me?" He bent forward, grabbed a hand-full of Tony's thick, black hair with his chubby fingers, pulled back sharply and spit in his face. "You were always telling me what to do. Weren't you? You had to be the boss. Didn't you? My old man thought he was the boss too. Right up until the time I bashed his head in with a crowbar. His body must have twitched for close to a half an hour after I beat him," Jimmy said, his lips curled into a eerie smile. "They never did find his body. Mom figured he ran off with some two-bit whore from Texas. Yeah, I've waited a long time for this day. A long fucking time."

Blood poured out onto the floor beside Tony's body and he began to loose consciousness. His outstretched arm lay harmlessly around Jimmy's feet. He tugged feebly on his pant cuffs.

"Oh here, let me wipe that blood from your face," Jimmy said, ramming the pointed toe of his boot into the side of Tony's head.

The agonizing pain of his teeth being ripped from his gums and his jaw splitting in half was the last thing Tony Molino would feel before he died.

Jimmy rolled him over, put the barrel of the gun a few inches from his face and fired twice. Tony's head exploded like a melon. Half of his brain splattered against the wall and floorboards and his body jerked one last time. Callahan stood over the body and watched a steady stream of blood flow across the floor and pool in the corner.

Robert eased back into the chair. Tony's gun was only a few feet away but Jimmy was much too erratic. A half a minute passed before Jimmy spoke again.

"Look at that, will you? I've got blood on my brand-new boots. Damn! It's going to stain the leather. It always does." He bent forward and activated the bomb. "It's nothing personal, gentlemen. I can't leave any loose ends for Jackson to find. I'm sure you can understand that. Can't you?" He slid the gun into his pants and stepped back. "I'm guessing he'll be here in the morning. It'll take the old man a while to figure out what happened and by then it'll be too late. I'll have sold your research and will be off to South America."

Jimmy picked up the backpack, swung it over his shoulder and checked his watch. "Well I really need to be going now," he said. "I suppose it would be really callous for me to say have a nice evening, so I won't. But at least you had the pleasure of watching Tony die first." He turned around and headed toward the door. "You've got less than two minutes to live. I'll see you in hell someday."

"Go to hell, motherfucker and keep looking over your shoulder because I'll be there one of these days. I swear to God I'll be there," Robert screamed.

Jimmy laughed and walked out the door. A few seconds later, the headlights of the Rambler pierced the darkness outside the warehouse and quickly disappeared into the night.

Robert sprung to his feet and began cutting through his father's ropes. "Where did you get the knife?" Edward asked.

"I carry it with me all the time. Had it since I was a kid. Actually, it used to belong to you." He sawed back and forth feverishly but the progress was slow. "Damn it, the knife's friggin' dull. Come on, come on, you son-of-a-bitch!" he yelled.

"Try the knots," Edward suggested.

"I already have. They'll take too long."

"Then leave me and get out of here."

"I'll carry you out on this chair if I have to. We leave together or not at all. I'm not about to lose you again."

"How much time is left?"

"Less than thirty seconds, but I'm almost through. We should make it with plenty of time to spare. Just a little longer now. Just a few more sec—there! That's it, let's go!"

The ropes fell to the ground. Robert yanked his father from the chair and they sprinted out the door. Suddenly he stopped. "My laptop, I've got to go back. I'm stuck here without it."

"There isn't enough time."

Robert turned and raced up the driveway. "Stay here. I'll be right back," he yelled as he disappeared into the warehouse. He ran into the darkened building, stumbling over debris and feeling his way along the wall. He found the table, tossed it aside, dropped to his hands and knees and crawled along the floor, searching blindly for the laptop. The ticking of the bomb's timer echoed in his ears.

"Where the hell is it? I don't have time for thi–Got it!" he yelled, pulling himself to his feet and racing toward the exit. He was less than ten feet from the door when he caught a foot on Molino's body and flew through the air, hitting his head on an iron post. His body went limp and everything went blank.

CHAPTER 20

The warehouse burst into a thousand pieces. Splinters of wood and glass rained down in every direction. A deafening explosion was followed by a huge billowing ball of fire that lit the evening sky for miles. Thick black smoke poured into the night, suffocating everything it touched. The metal girders that supported the roof quickly gave way under the intense heat, and falling debris ignited several nearby buildings. The sound of emergency sirens filled the air.

A few seconds passed before the blurriness faded and Robert's eyes came into focus. He woke to find his father sitting beside him, cradling his head in his lap and keeping the blood from dripping into his eyes.

"How are you feeling?" Edward asked.

"How do I look?" Robert moaned.

"Like shit."

"That's just about how I feel. My head's pounding. Feels like I got a jackhammer in there," he complained, holding his hands over his eyes. He tried sitting up but was only able to lift his head a few inches. "What happened? Last thing I remember is cutting your ropes."

"You ran inside for the laptop and hit your head on one of the supports. I found you laying on the floor a few feet from Molino's body."

"Jesus! The laptop—"

"Relax. I've got it right here."

"Thank God. I'd be finished without it. Thanks for saving my life." Robert turned his head and looked over toward what was left of the warehouse. "A hell of a fire, isn't it? I bet you can see it from across the lake. We've got to get out of here before the police arrive."

"Just lay still. You may have a concussion. We've got to get you to the hospital," Edward said, restraining his son.

"No way! Jimmy thinks we're dead and we've got to make sure he keeps thinking that. At least until we can catch up with him. He's got the rest of my equipment and I've got to get it back before he leaves town. Besides, what are we going to say to the police? They'll want to know who I am and what we're doing here. Help me to my feet. We've got to find a phone."

Neither man heard the car inching up the driveway behind them until it was too late. "It's Jimmy. Let's get out of here," Robert yelled.

They sprinted toward the trees as fast as they could, neither looked back. Not even when they heard the car door slam or the rhythmic sound of feet hitting the ground and laying chase.

We've got a chance if we can make it to the trees. It will be dark. There will be places to hide, Robert thought.

They continued to race toward the inviting safety of the woods. The ground was muddy and slick. Thick brush tugged at their skin, scrapping and cutting as they darted through it. They ran as fast as their legs would carry them; jumping over fallen logs, leaping across ditches, dodging small trees and rocks. The tree line was less than twenty yards away when Robert planted his foot on a wet rock, twisted an ankle, and lost his footing. He tumbled to the ground, flipped head-over-heels and smashed a knee against a boulder. A dog's bark pierced the night and a flashlight beam illuminated the ground around him. He could hear the animal's rapid panting and mashing of the brush as it rushed toward him. He looked back and saw the silhouette of man following close behind, zigzagging through the rugged terrain. His flashlight bobbed up and down with each step he took. Robert frantically tried to stand but his leg wouldn't take the weight. "Dad, get out of here! I won't make it. My leg's shot," he yelled.

Edward grabbed his son by the arm and pulled. "Get up, you're going to make it even if I have to—"

"Hey, Finaldi! It's okay. It's me, Charlie Moore."

Casey was straddling Robert a second later, licking the mud from his face.

"You look like hell, doc," Charlie said, shining the flashlight on his battered face. "Whose fist did you run into?"

Robert cupped his hand over his eyes, shielding himself from the glare of the light. "It's good to see you too. What are you doing here?"

"I was at the airport and saw Molino and Callahan shove the two of you into their car. I followed for a while but lost you after they exited onto Seneca Street. I got caught at a train crossing and when the tracks finally cleared…the Rambler was nowhere to be found. I've been driving around for an hour looking for you and was just about to give up when I saw the fire. I figured it'd have something to do with you. Although, to tell you the truth, I wasn't expecting to find either of you alive. How did you manage to escape?"

"It's a long story that we don't have time for. We've got to get out of here. Can you take us back to my hotel? We need to regroup. Jimmy's out there and we need to find him before he leaves the city. He's got half of my equipment and two years of Edward's research. We need to get them back before he has a chance to sell them."

                    *   *   *

"You know, I've lived most of my life in this town but I've never set foot inside a room at the Roycroft before," Charlie said, surveying the surroundings. "Not too shabby, not too shabby at all. Do you mind if I peruse the patio, doc?"

Robert nodded. "Sure, help yourself. Just don't steal anything," he joked.

"How are we going to find him? Jimmy could be anywhere by now," Edward asked.

"We need to see what flights depart for South America tomorrow and stake out the airport. He'll probably leave on the first available flight in the morning. Let's just hope there aren't any red-eye flights out of here tonight or we're screwed."

Robert grabbed the phone book and tossed it to his father. "Would you look up the airlines and read off the numbers? I'll call."

Charlie stepped back into the room and sat on the bed. "Hey, doc, do you mind if I turn on the tube? The Ed Sullivan Show's on in a few minutes and I never miss it."

"Sure, go ahead."

Edward mumbled to himself as he thumbed through the yellow pages. "Let's try Pan American first. They fly the majority of the international flights out of Buffalo."

"Sounds good, what's their—"

"Holy shit! I don't believe it. He's dead. Kennedy's dead!" Charlie interrupted.

Robert dropped the phone and rushed to the television. "Turn it up! Turn it all the way up!" he yelled.

We have just received word that presidential candidate John Fitzgerald Kennedy is dead. I repeat, Senator John F. Kennedy died in an airplane crash earlier this evening. His campaign manager has confirmed that he was a passenger on a small commuter flight which was bound for Boston. The twin engine aircraft crashed in the mountains, near a small Appalachian town, northeast of Albany. We have reports from rescue crews at the remote crash site that the Senator's body has been recovered and positively identified. Preliminary reports indicate that there were no survivors. The cause

*of the crash is unknown at this time but believed to be engine fail-
ure. Again, reliable sources have—*

"Jimmy wasn't lying," Edward said.

Robert lowered his head into his hands. "My God! What the hell have
I done. He wasn't supposed to die. Not yet. Not until Dallas. How could
I have been so stupid? Michael was right. I should never have come
back."

"What is it? What's wrong?" his father asked.

"Kennedy wasn't supposed to die in a plane crash. He wasn't even
suppose to be on board. He was on stand-by. I stopped you from boarding and he must have taken your seat."

"You mind telling me what's going on?" Charlie asked.

Robert turned the laptop on and waited anxiously for it to power-up.
"I need to see just how much damage I've done."

"What's going on? Are you a Fed or something? I hear they got all
sorts of gadgets like that. Real James Bond type of stuff," Charlie said,
staring at the blue computer screen.

The laptop finally booted-up and Robert slid the CD into the drive.
"I'll run a comparison between the CD and the copy I installed on the
hard drive before I came back. Any differences should come up on the
screen in a few seconds."

"You lost me, doc. Differences in what?"

"Trust me on this one, Charlie, you wouldn't believe me if I told—"

Robert froze. He stared in disbelief at the information on the computer screen in front of him. It was worse than he could have imagined.
Much worse!

CHAPTER 21

Light rain began to fall at the Buffalo Airport a few minutes after Daniel Jackson's private jet touched down on runway nine. Its passengers quickly deplaned under the cover of darkness and were shuttled into the waiting limousine.

Patrick O'Brien, the driver, was a big, gabby, red-haired kid who grew up in the heart of Buffalo's Irish community. He was the kind of kid everyone liked, always willing to lend a hand or a dollar to someone in need.

"Welcome to Buffalo, Mr. Jackson. Looks like you brought the rain with you. It just started coming down a few minutes ago. We'd be looking at snow if it were a dozen degrees cooler. I imagine you don't see much of the white stuff in Houston, huh? So where would you like me to take you?" Patrick asked, adjusting the rearview mirror so he could get a better look at his passengers.

A thin, grey-haired man, sandwiched between two large bodyguards, leaned forward. "I need to go to the Statler Hotel on Delaware. Do you know where it is?" he asked in a monotone voice.

"Sure do, my father worked there part-time, a few years after it opened in forty-four. He'd bring me to work with him every Saturday morning. Boy! Does that bring back memories. I remember when this real fat lady and her pencil thin husband walked into the—"

"Just drive me to the fucking hotel and shut-up. I don't give a shit about your father's job or how you spent your friggin' weekends. I don't want to hear how you used to jerk-off in the coat room while you were drooling over playboy magazines," Jackson barked, sliding back in between his bodyguards and lighting a cigar.

Patrick drove the twenty minutes to the hotel without saying another word or looking in the rearview mirror again.

★   ★   ★

"Turn off the lights and drive around to the rear," Jackson ordered. "This will do nicely, stop right here," he said as the car pulled into a discrete alleyway behind the hotel. "Okay gentlemen, time to find Molino and Callahan. Tommy, I want you to go inside. Check with the clerk and find out what room they're in. Rico, you and Michael locate the freight elevator and have it waiting for me. Check the basement and see if their car's there, Johnny," Jackson said from the back seat, sitting with his legs crossed and puffing on his cigar. Patrick O'Brien sat silently in the driver's seat wishing he'd stayed home.

Tommy returned a few minutes later and climbed into the limo. "They're in room six-twenty-four, Mr. Jackson. The clerk said he hasn't seen either of them all night and he's been working since three this afternoon."

Johnny tapped on the car window and waited for it to be lowered. "Their car's parked in the basement and I didn't see anything inside of it. The doors were locked. You want me to break in?"

Jackson shook his head. "No, let's see what Tony and Jimmy have to say first. I want to know why they haven't called."

★   ★   ★

"What's wrong?" Edward asked.

"There's nothing on the disk after October 25, 1962, nothing at all. It's supposed to contain all of the major news stories from 1960 to 1983. The year I left."

Edward leaned forward and read the computer screen. "What are you saying?"

"What do you mean, you left in 1983?" Charlie asked nervously.

"In the fall of 1962, less than two years from now, the CIA will discover a Soviet built nuclear missile base in Cuba. History will remember it as the Cuban Missile Crisis. The base is only a few weeks away from being fully operational by the time it's detected. Needless to say, the U.S. could never adequately defend against a missile launch from Cuba. The air to ground travel time is much too short. We wouldn't have time to scramble a jet, much less shoot the missiles down. Miami would be toast in less time than it takes to cook an egg. That missile base posed the most significant threat to our country since World War II. A nuclear launch from Cuba would make Pearl Harbor seem like a walk in the park," Robert explained. Edward and Charlie stood alongside him and listened.

"Kennedy wasn't supposed to die today. He was supposed to win the presidential election next month. But all that changed when I stopped you from boarding the plane. With Kennedy gone, Nixon wins the election in a landslide. He handles the Cuban Missile Crisis much more aggressively than Kennedy. He believes that the U.S. can win a limited nuclear war and responds to the threat by launching a preemptive nuclear attack on major Soviet cities and military targets. The Soviets, of course, respond in-kind. Nixon was wrong. There is no such thing as a limited nuclear war. Hundreds of millions of people die within hours and a half billion more within a week. All this happens because of my decision to stop you from getting on the plane." He turned the computer off, stood and stared at his father. "I've just killed millions of innocent people. Their blood is on my hands."

"You couldn't have known this would happen," Edward said.

"I saw JFK at the airport but never gave it a second thought. How could have I been so damn stupid?"

Edward placed a hand on his son's shoulder. "You'll have to send me back so I can get on the plane. You've got no choice."

Robert looked at his father and turned away. "You can't go back. No one can. Jimmy's got part of the equipment I need. We're dead in the water without it."

"Excuse me, I don't mean to interrupt, but just what the hell is going on? How can you know what happens in the future?" Charlie asked. He was nervous, scared, and needed a drink.

"I don't have the time to try and convince you so I'm just going to say this once. It's up to you whether or not you believe me. But no matter what you think or how you feel…we need you. Don't quit on us now, all I'm asking for is another twenty-four hours of your time. If we don't catch Jimmy before he leaves nothing else will matter."

    *   *   *

Tommy methodically rolled a toothpick from one corner of his mouth to the other, flipping it with his tongue and slowly working it back to the other side of his mouth again. "No one's answering the door," he reported casually.

"Pick the lock," Jackson ordered without hesitation.

Within seconds, eight men, with guns drawn, were rummaging through the vacant hotel room.

Tommy walked out of one of the bedrooms carrying a padlocked wooden box. "Tony's things are still here but Jimmy's room is clean as a whistle. Looks like the bastard split. I found this box hidden under a blanket in Tony's closet. The lock's a piece of crap. I'll have it open in no time."

"Hey, boss. There's an envelope addressed to you. It was laying on the counter, next to the phone," Johnny yelled from across the room.

Daniel Jackson tore the envelope open while Tommy worked on the lock a few feet away.

Dear Mr. Jackson:

By the time you read this letter I'll be long gone. I'm sure even a stupid piece-of-shit like YOU has figured out by now that I've sold Paolucci's work to someone else. Don't bother looking for Paolucci or Tony. All that's left are ashes. Killing Tony gave me great satisfaction. Too bad you weren't there to join him.

I wish I could see the look on your ugly, wrinkled face but I can't have everything. I'll enjoy spending your money, though.

Kiss my ass,

Jimmy

P.S. Would you mind picking up the hotel bill? I had to leave in a hurry.

"Find that fat, son-of-a-bitch and bring him to me! Alive!" Jackson demanded, pounding his fist on the counter. "I want him found tonight!"

Tommy clicked the last tumbler on the lock and opened the wooded box. "Hey, Mr. Jackson, the fat bastard left another note." He unfolded the paper and read the note out loud.

"Bend over and kiss your sorry ass goodbye...hmm. I don't get—"

"Get out of here!" Jackson yelled as he sprinted to the door.

An explosion ripped through the hotel room a split second later and when the dust settled, only four men, including Daniel Jackson, walked out alive. Tommy never had a chance. A leg and half an arm, buried beneath the rubble, were all the police would find of him.

        *   *   *

Edward tossed the phone book back in the drawer. "That's it, that's the last airline. There aren't any flights out of here tonight. First one's on Delta at six. What do we do now? Wait?"

"What do you think, Charlie?" Robert asked.

"I think I need a drink," Charlie replied. He walked to the bed and sat down. "I'm not sure what to think or believe anymore. Hell, I'm just a dumb old farm-boy. All of this is way too weird for me."

"Forget about all the stuff I just told you. You have to put that aside for now. How would you normally handle this type of a case?"

Charlie thought for a moment. "I wouldn't put all my eggs in one basket. I wouldn't wait for the flight. I'd go looking for him tonight."

Robert nodded. "I agree. Where do we start?"

"Back at my office. I have a file on him and Molino. Let's see if it will lead us anywhere."

Edward grabbed his coat off the top of the dresser. "Great, let's go," he said, opening the door.

*   *   *

Casey bounded up the steps leading to the office and patiently waited at the door. His tail wagged a little faster with each step Charlie took.

"Come in, fellas. It ain't much to look at, Edward, but it gets the job done. Have a seat while I rustle up the paperwork on our fat friend."

Robert popped open a desk drawer, pulled out a dog biscuit and tossed it across the room. Casey snatched it in midair, trotted to the corner and chewed it in private.

"I wish I could see your mother one last time. I was so rushed. I never had much of a chance to say goodbye. I hope she's all right," Edward said.

Robert pulled up a chair and sat next to him. "For the first couple of months after the crash I kept waiting for you to walk through the door before dinner. Just like you always did. I'd sit in the chair by the front door and stare out the window. Hoping the next car that turned the corner would be yours. Mom let me sit there for a while and never said anything about it. She stayed in the kitchen, getting dinner ready. Once in awhile, for the first few months, she'd forget and put three settings on the table. I think there were days she half-expected you to walk through the door too. She really loved you. Still does."

*   *   *

The limousine's tires scrapped up against the curb as it came to a stop outside Charlie's office.

"That must be it there, Mr. Jackson. The building with the light on."

"What's this private dick's name?" Jackson asked coldly.

"Charlie Moore," Johnny responded promptly. "I don't know much about him. Tommy was working the case."

Daniel Jackson puffed on his cigar and stared out the window. The rain had slowed to a mist and the air was still. "Tommy was a good man. A damn good man. I'm the godfather of one of his kids. That fat bastard is going to pay. I'll see to that. He'll fucking pay all right. Let's go say hello to Mr. Moore."

*   *   *

"There's not a whole lot of information to go on. Callahan was a real enigma. He scored much higher than normal on IQ tests. A surveillance and demolition expert who couldn't cut it in the military. He looks like your typical middle-age guy next door. The kind of guy you'd let your kids play with. There's nothing sinister looking about him at all. He's the kind of guy who was probably picked on all his life. You know the type, always turning over his lunch money to the class bully. Too afraid to run and not tough enough to fight."

Charlie sat down at his desk, put his feet up and skimmed the report. "But make no mistake about it, there's an evil inside of him, something that burns just below the surface."

"Yeah we know. We've been there during a meltdown and it's scary. Real scary," Edward said.

"What does a guy like him do in his spare time? Do you know if he had a girlfriend up here?" Robert asked.

Charlie laughed. "No girlfriends. That's for sure, doc."

"How do you know?"

Charlie cleared his throat. "Cause he's a faggot!"

"Jimmy's gay?" Robert asked.

"Queer as a three-dollar bill. A little *light* in the loafers as they say. I bet the poor bastard's never slept with a woman in his life."

Robert jumped up. "Where are the gay bars in Buffalo? He's been cooped up with Tony for months and probably hasn't had a chance to get out by himself. I bet that son-of-a-bitch is out celebrating tonight."

"There's a gay bar on the corner of Allen and Elmwood"

Robert smiled, looked at Charlie and raised an eyebrow. "Hmm…and just how do you know that?" he joked.

"I umm…worked on this case for a woman who thought her husband had a girlfriend on the side," Charlie explained awkwardly. "She was surprised as hell to find out about his boyfriend. Shit! You see everything in this business. Nothing surprises me. Not anymore."

Casey snapped his head toward the stairs and growled. It was the kind of noise dogs make when they mean business. The kind of noise that you don't ignore.

Charlie swung his feet down, grabbed his gun from the drawer and crawled over to the window. "We've got company. I count four men in all. It's too dark to make out their faces." He sat up, leaned against the wall, pulled a box of bullets off the desk, and poured them into his pocket. "I don't like the looks of this. Four men in suits, this late at night. Something's going down. We better slip out the back."

Charlie snapped a leash onto Casey's collar and they crawled on the floor to the rear window. "Let's hope there aren't four more out back. Stay close to me. There's a trail that winds through the fields, it will take us out to the Hadley farm. I'll drop Casey off there and borrow the old man's truck. You go first, doc. Edward, you're second. I'll lower Casey down after you," he whispered.

*   *   *

Daniel Jackson and two of his men were knocking at the front door as Robert slid out the back window headfirst. He was just starting to get to his feet when he felt the cold barrel of a gun press against his cheek. Charlie crouched down and signaled for Edward to hold up. He clicked the safety off his pistol and listened.

"It's a little late for a fire drill. Don't you think, mister? Now get to your feet. Nice and slow. Don't do anything stupid. Screw with me and I'll cap you right here," Johnny said.

Robert slowly rose to his feet, grabbing hold of a baseball sized rock without Johnny noticing.

"Hey, Mr. Jackson, I caught a guy sneaking out the back window. Probably the private dick you're looking for. I'll bring the prick up front in a second," Johnny yelled.

Casey wiggled out of Edward's grasp, ran to the window and barked. Johnny turned toward the noise. Robert moved quickly. He struck Johnny in the side of the head with the rock, opening a three-inch gash across his forehead, just below the hair line. Johnny was stunned, but only for a second. He pointed his pistol at Robert and slowly rose to his feet. Blood spilled over his eyebrow and dripped into his eye. He reached up and wiped it away.

"Bad move, asshole. You're going to die for that!" Johnny put the gun against his head and cocked the hammer. Robert spun, pivoted on one foot and kicked the pistol cleanly from his hand. A second kick caught

Johnny in the ribs and sent him sprawling to the ground. Johnny managed to lift his head up just in time to see the bottom of Robert's shoe before it crashed into his face, crumpling his nose against his cheek. Blood rushed from his nostrils. He lost consciousness before he hit the ground.

"Let's get out of here before the rest of them get back here," Robert said, helping his father through the window.

They rested by a tree stump on the outskirts of the Hadley Farm and caught their breath a few minutes later.

"Christ! Where did you learn to do that? I've never seen anyone handle a man that easily."

Robert placed his foot on the tree stump and tied his laces tight. "I was a skinny ten-year-old kid who got picked on by the class bully, Tommy Henderson, a lot. My mom enrolled me in karate lessons after I came home with my third black-eye of the semester. I took my last lesson ten years later."

"What happened to Tommy Henderson?" Edward asked.

"His dad got transferred to Alabama when I was eleven and I never saw him again. A cousin of his said he died in a car crash a couple of years later. Said he had enough moonshine in his blood to kill a cow."

"I don't think they're following us but we better hurry and get to the farm just the same," Charlie said, rising to his feet.

"That goon back there thought I was you, Charlie. They probably think that Edward and I are dead, that's why they came looking for you. I bet they don't know where Jimmy is and they're hoping you can help. Let's hope we find him before Jackson."

CHAPTER 22

Jimmy's room at the Lafayette Hotel was anything but plush. The bathroom faucet leaked. The tub drained slowly. Radiators barely kept the small room warm and the worn cotton sheets hadn't been laundered in more than a week. Amenities were few and far between. But for the one night he planned on staying it was perfect—inconspicuous and out of the way. No one paid attention to anyone or anything and no questions were asked. The hotel was a haven for run-of-the-mill thieves, small time thugs, and prostitutes. Unsuspecting tourists, enticed by dirt cheap rates, usually lasted a night or less.

Jimmy splashed on cologne and adjusted his necktie in the cracked bathroom mirror. His blue and red striped tie didn't match his tan sports coat or black slacks, but neither did his belt or shoes.

"Yes sir, Jimmy. You're looking good. Looking *real* good! Time to go out and have some fun," he said to himself.

He took a chair from the kitchen. Dragged it to an area just outside the bathroom and stood on it. He lifted a ceiling tile up, exposing a metal strongbox containing Edward's notes and Robert's equipment. A small explosive device, a third the size of a shoe box, sat two feet in front of the metal box. The front half of the device was angled downward toward the floor and was crammed full of razor-sharp metal shavings, small nails and glass. The smaller rear compartment contained a tightly packed mixture of zinc powder and sulfur. Its reinforced-steel rear plate was specifically designed to direct a blast downward. Jimmy had painstakingly designed the explosive charge to kill or incapacitate intruders while minimizing damage to strongbox. Unfortunately, he never noticed the gas line that ran along a nearby joist and down the bathroom wall. He connected the red and green wires, attached the yellow lead to a pressure-activated switch and carefully put the ceiling tile back into place. The tripping mechanism, rigged with a seven-second delay, was virtually impossible to detect.

*   *   *

"Okay gentlemen, next stop Allen and Elmwood," Charlie said as he turned the ignition and backed Hadley's pickup truck out of the driveway. Casey sat alongside old man Hadley on the porch and watched the red truck disappear behind the barn before turning onto the dirt access road. "We should be there in forty-five minutes, give or take a few."

"What are we going to do if we find him? We just can't walk into a bar and drag him out kicking and screaming," Edward pointed out.

"I don't know about that, it sounds like a good plan to me," Robert joked. Air rushed into the truck as it picked up speed, Robert pushed his hair back away from his eyes. The cool night air stung his battered face. "What do you think, Charlie, how should we handle the fat man?"

Charlie turned the truck onto the Aurora Expressway and slid over to the passing lane. "The old-fashioned way. We'll flush him out. I guess I draw the short straw seeing that he'd recognize the two of you. I'll go into the bar and look for him while the two of you cover the exits."

"I don't know, Charlie, can we trust you not to do a little cruising while you're in there?" Edward cracked.

"Hmm, you may have something there. He does seem a bit eager to go in now that you mention it," Robert added, patting the private detective on the back and smiling.

"Boys, let me tell you something right here and right now! I may be a lot of things, but I assure you that there's not a homosexual cell in my body."

"Yeah, yeah, we've heard it all before," Edward joked.

"We're just busting on you, Charlie. My college roommate was gay. It's no big deal," Robert added.

"You'll be fine. Just remember to keep your back to the wall," Edward teased.

"Don't worry I will, and I know…don't drop the soap," Charlie laughed as he pressed down on the clutch and slid the truck into over-drive.

*   *   *

The Dark Room was a fitting name for the bar which sat behind a laundromat on the corner of Allen and Elmwood Streets. A small unlit sign stood atop the front doorjamb and, other than the street address, was the building's only marking. Few patrons used the front door at all. Most were regulars and knew about the discreet alleyway that led from Park Street to the back door. A gas streetlight provided just enough light for most to maneuver down the narrow brick walkway. The black paint on the windows was thick enough to keep most of the light out and more importantly, to keep anyone from seeing inside.

Jimmy sat at a corner table with Frank, a regular fixture at the bar. He was young, good looking, and always looking for a free drink. He didn't have a steady job or a regular place to live and had been on his own ever since his father caught him in the attic with another boy when he was sixteen.

Callahan had only been in the bar for an hour and Frank had already hit him up for four drinks. Jimmy didn't mind. He figured it would take a few more to get Frank back to his hotel room.

"So where did you say you were from again?" Frank asked for the second time, badly slurring his words.

Jimmy slid another drink in front of him. "Houston Texas," he repeated. "Here you go, have another. You're a couple behind me."

"Don't mind if I do. Aren't you going to join me?"

"I've got one coming. Why don't you get started? Mine should be here any minute now."

"Cheers," Frank said, lifting the glass up over his head and pouring half the drink down his throat. "I lived in Fort Worth for a few years. My old man was assigned there before he went overseas. I've never been to Houston though. To tell you the truth I don't remember much of Texas. We moved around so much that after a while all the bases looked the same."

*   *   *

"Why are you pulling over? There's nothing here but a laundromat," Edward said.

"See that building behind the laundromat?" Charlie said.

"Yeah."

"That's the Dark Room. It's the only gay bar in the city. If Jimmy's not in there then we're back to square one."

"Same plan as before?" Robert asked.

"Yep, I'll go in and check the place out. You cover the back and Edward will stay put just in case he slips past me. Remember, he knows both of you by sight so stay in the shadows. If the asshole comes out the front door blow on the horn a couple of times. I'll come running."

*   *   *

"I'll be back in a minute. I've got to take a leak. Here's a twenty to cover my drink." Callahan moved his chair aside and walked to the bathroom just as Charlie sat down at the bar.

"What can I do you for, mate?" the bartender asked.

"I'm just here for a drink, pal. Nothing else," Charlie said nervously.

"Relax man. Take it easy. First time in a gay bar or what?"

Charlie lifted his baseball cap up, ran his fingers through his hair and leaned back in the chair. "Sorry, I'm just a little jumpy that's all. Too much coffee I guess. I'll have a shot of Jack, straight-up," he said, placing the cap back on his head. "Come to think of it, make it a double. Will you?" Charlie swivelled on the bar stool and scanned the room.

No sign of Jimmy, he thought.

"Not much of a crowd tonight, huh?" he asked.

"It usually picks up a little later. Half of the guys that come in here are married. They wait for their wives to go to bed and then head downtown." The bartender laid a tumbler down on the bar and filled it with whiskey.

Charlie nodded and looked around the bar again before scooping up the glass and gulping down the whiskey. "Ah, now that's what I call whiskey. Damn good whiskey!" he said gritting his teeth. "There's nothing quite like Jack, now is there? Double me up again, bartender?"

"Sure thing, mate. Hold on a second. Hey, Joey, do me a favor and run this over to Frank's table. It's for the fat guy he's with tonight."

Charlie watched Joey thread his way through the crowd, stopping every so often to pick up additional orders. He finally made it to Jimmy's table and put the drink down in front of the empty chair next to Frank. Charlie sipped on his whiskey while keeping an eye on the table. He slowly reached under his jacket, popped the strap on his holster, and pushed the safety in on his revolver.

"He's good-looking but dumb as a box of rocks," the bartender commented.

"Huh, what did you say?" Charlie asked, still keeping his eyes trained on the empty chair.

"Frank, the guy you're staring at over there, sitting by himself in the corner. He's a looker all right but not much upstairs."

What the hell am I doing here? Charlie thought.

✴   ✴   ✴

Robert pulled his collar tight to his neck and folded his arms across his chest, trying to keep warm. As he crouched down behind a set of shrubs just outside the rear door, he realized just how tired and sore he was. His ankle and knee were badly bruised and swollen. His shoulder had finally stopped bleeding and his face felt as though it had been run over by a truck. And if all that wasn't bad enough he had a thundering headache to deal with.

What's taking Charlie so long? he thought.

✴   ✴   ✴

"Ah, that feels better. Now I have room for a few more drinks. I see they finally brought over my manhattan," Jimmy said, returning to the table.

"Yeah, Joey dropped it off a minute ago," Frank answered, never offering Jimmy the change from his twenty.

Jimmy squeezed into the chair, pushing the table forward with his gut. "Whew, it sure is a tight fit. Isn't it, Franky?"

Frank didn't respond. Instead, he looked up at the man standing behind Jimmy.

Callahan felt the firm grip of a cold hand on his shoulder and warm breath on his neck. He could smell the fresh scent of whiskey lingering in the air.

"Keep both hands on the table and tell Frank to take a hike," Charlie whispered as he pressed the barrel of his gun against Jimmy's ribs.

"And if I don't? What are you going to do? Shoot me right here in front of Frank and everyone else?"

Charlie squeezed hard on Jimmy's shoulder. "Push me and find out. Now tell the little fag he needs to leave. He needs to leave right now!"

"Hey, is this guy bothering you?" Frank asked, slurring most of his words.

"It's all right, Frank. Why don't you leave us alone for a few minutes?"

Frank muttered something under his breath, stood up and stumbled to the bar. Charlie watched him for a few seconds before pulling up a chair and sitting across the table from Callahan.

"Who are you? And what do you want with me?" Jimmy asked. There was a slight quiver in his voice and small beads of sweat began forming on his forehead.

"Do what I tell you and I won't kill you. We're going to stand up and walk out the front door in a few seconds. You need to keep your mouth shut and hands at your sides. I'll have a gun pressed into the small of your back and won't hesitate to drop you if you're stupid enough to mess with me." Charlie's voice was firm and certain.

"I'll pay you ten times whatever you're getting from Jackson. All you have to do is let me go. Tell him you couldn't find me. There's nothing to it." Jimmy reached toward his vest pocket. "I've got the money right—"

"Put your hand down and don't move it again! You move when I tell you to move. You talk when I tell you to talk. Otherwise shut-up and sit still, asshole. I'm not working for Jackson. I don't work for scum and I'm not interested in your money. If I were, I'd cap you right here and take it." He grabbed Jimmy's drink and poured it in his mouth, swallowing it in a single gulp. "Now, Mr. Callahan, get up slowly, walk to the door, and keep your big mouth shut. Is that clear?"

Jimmy nodded and slowly rose to his feet, pretending not to notice Frank and a bouncer quickly approaching from behind.

"Is there a problem here?" the bouncer asked.

Charlie took a few steps back and turned his head, keeping his back to the wall, and an eye on Jimmy. "This doesn't concern you, I suggest you back off, pal."

"I wasn't talking to you, pal! I was talking to Jimmy."

Charlie pulled his pistol out from under his jacket. "You've got five seconds to back off and get out of my face. I'm taking fat boy with me so tell Frank he'll have to find another dick to suck tonight. Now back up and —"

Jimmy flipped the table and sprinted toward the back door. The bouncer pounced on Charlie, driving him hard to the floor, knocking the pistol from his hand. Frank ran to the bar to call the police.

Charlie took a couple of quick blows to the face before he was able to recover. He freed an arm, reached through the bouncer's stocky arms, and grabbed hold of his throat.

*   *   *

Callahan exploded through the back door and was ten steps down the alley before Robert had a chance to react. He leaped after him and caught just enough of Jimmy's heel to send him tumbling to the ground. He was on him a split-second later. The two men rolled viciously back and forth in the narrow alleyway, scraping against the jagged brick walls. Each tried to gain control. Jimmy was quicker and stronger than Robert had anticipated and managed to get to his feet first. Robert took two kicks to the stomach and one to the head before he managed to grab hold of Jimmy's foot. He stood up, still clutching Callahan's ankle. The side of his face was numb and his ribs ached with each breath.

"Surprised to see me?" Robert said, kicking Jimmy's leg out from under him, sending him crashing to the ground. He bent over, pulled him close, and drove his fist sharply into his face. Jimmy could feel the cartilage in his nose crumble.

"What's the matter, asshole? Cat got your tongue?" Robert grabbed what he could of Jimmy's thinning hair and jammed the back of his head into the bricks. "You're going to tell me where my equipment is or

I'll split your head open!" He made a fist and drew back his arm. Jimmy covered his face and braced for a beating.

"Well, fat-ass, what's it going to be? I'll give you something you never gave me...a chance. Now, for the last time. Where's the equipment?"

Jimmy looked up. His lips curled into an infuriatingly smug smile.

"All right. We do it the hard—"

The garden hose closed around Robert's neck before he had a chance to get a hand underneath it. Frank tightened his grip and leaned back against the railing, using all of his weight to choke off his air.

      *   *   *

The bouncer stopped punching just long enough to peel Charlie's hands from his throat, giving him the break he desperately needed. Charlie jammed a thumb deep into his eye. The bouncer reeled backwards, screaming in pain. Charlie didn't hesitate. He sprung to his feet and quickly landed two punches to the head. The big man staggered for a second and slumped forward. Charlie picked up a chair, smashed it over his back, and watched him drop to the floor. He grabbed the back of his head and slammed it into the floorboards.

      *   *   *

Robert was quickly losing consciousness. Jimmy got to his feet and picked up a scrap piece of lumber.

"That's it, Jimmy, do it! Do it now! Beat him senseless! I've got him real tight. The bastard's got no air. He ain't going nowhere. Lay into him real good!" Frank screamed.

Jimmy smiled, drew the board back and took a step forward. Robert pushed back hard, shifting all his weight onto Frank, and sent a kick into Callahan's mid-section, driving him to his knees. Robert moved quickly. He reached back, grabbed hold of Frank's hair and pulled as hard as he could. Jimmy staggered to his feet, picked up the lumber, and swung wildly. Robert sent an elbow crashing into Frank's chest and dropped to his knees. Frank didn't have a chance. The end of the lumber smashed into his neck, shattering his collar. A protruding nail cut deeply into his flesh, tearing a foot long gash from the top of his shoulder to the bottom of his chest. Frank's agonizing scream echoed in the alleyway as he collapsed into a whimpering broken mass on the staircase. Jimmy didn't flinch, he drew back the bloody lumber again. But this time he was a split second too late. Robert leg-whipped him and sent him tumbling to the ground. He stood over Callahan, stepped on his arm, and kicked the piece of wood away. He dropped to his knees, straddled him and began pounding him with his fists. Hitting him over and over again. He quickly turned Jimmy's face into a bloody pulp.

"I think he's had enough," Charlie said, grabbing hold of Robert's arm. "We need to get out of here before the police arrive or we'll be spending the night in the holding center. Come on, doc, this isn't your style. Remember the big picture. We've got work to do."

CHAPTER 23

"You better not be lying, Jimmy. I've had a hell of a night already thanks to you." Robert tightened his grip on Callahan's arm, squeezing deep into the fat surrounding his triceps.

"Hey! Take it easy! That hurts! I'm telling you the truth. Everything's in there, you'll see."

"Here we are, room two-oh-four," Charlie said, handing the key to Jimmy. "Open the door. I want it to be your dick that gets blown off if you've booby-trapped it. Turn the key, push the door open, and don't go inside until I tell you."

Charlie looked in both directions, making sure the hallway was clear. He drew his pistol and signaled for Jimmy to put the key into the lock. "Easy does it now. Nice and slow."

Jimmy fumbled with the key before clumsily sliding it into the lock. He paused until Charlie nodded and then slowly pushed the door open, sending it into the darkness of the room. The eerie creaking of the brass hinges terminated with an echoing thud as the doorknob came to rest against the plaster wall.

Charlie held Callahan by the neck and pushed him into the room with the Paoluccis following close behind.

"It's dark in here, hit the lights will you—"

A floor lamp in the far corner clicked on before Charlie could finish his sentence.

"Come in, gentlemen and would you be so kind as to close the door behind you? This hotel is filled with vagrants and reprobates. It's completely unsafe," Daniel Jackson said, stepping out of the shadows. An unlit cigar dangled from his mouth. Charlie Moore felt the barrel of a sawed-off shotgun press up against his ribs just as a hand reached out and took his pistol. Edward and Robert were thrown against the wall and frisked while two of Jackson's men pushed Jimmy into the kitchen and held a gun to his head.

"They're clean, boss," Johnny said, shoving Robert and his father headfirst into the sofa. Charlie joined them a moment later.

Jackson walked over and sat down on a coffee table in front of the sofa. He looked at Edward and smiled. A cigar was still wedged between his yellow teeth. "I'm pleased, although somewhat surprised, to see that you're still alive, Professor. Now, which one of your friends is Finaldi and which one's Moore?"

Edward didn't reply.

"Let's not make this more difficult than it has to be. All I'm asking for you to do is point them out. I have to warn you that I've had a fucking bad day and my patience is a little thin. It would behoove you to cooperate."

"I'm Finaldi," Robert volunteered. "Who are you?"

Jackson lit his cigar and smiled. "Hey Johnny, which one of these gentlemen did you encounter in the alley behind Moore's office earlier this evening?"

Johnny swung his shotgun up from his side and held it to Robert's forehead. "That's the motherfucker."

"I think you know who I am, Dr. Finaldi, and you can rest assured that I'll find out who you really are and what you're doing here before the night's through. Johnny will see to it. By the way, I didn't know they taught hand-to-hand combat at Cornell. Was it an elective?"

"It's a hobby of mine. I taught myself," Robert answered tersely. Jackson laughed and took a long puff on his cigar. "A hobby, huh? I think it's important for a man to have a hobby. I have hobbies, isn't that right, Jimmy?" He took off his grey suitcoat, tossed it on the coffee table, and walked to the kitchen. "Looks like someone did a number on your face," he said, turning Callahan's head from side-to-side. "I think they even busted your nose. Looks like Finaldi's handiwork."

Jimmy didn't answer. Beads of sweat formed on his forehead and upper lip.

"Let me see now. I believe the last time I heard from you, you left a rather crass note telling me to kiss your fat-ass. Do you remember?"

Jimmy remained silent.

Jackson slowly walked behind him. "You have something that belongs to me and I'm only going to ask you for it once. You won't get a second chance." Jimmy could feel his warm breath on the back of his neck. "Where are the notes?"

"Screw you! You're going to kill me whether I tell you or not, so why don't you just cap me now and get it over with?"

Jackson stepped back in front of him and smirked. "That's what I like about you, Jimmy, you're a smart guy, and you're right. I'm going to kill you whether you tell me or not. The difference is that I'll torture you if you don't. If you're smart and tell me, I'll make it quick. One shot behind the ear. You won't feel a thing."

"I'll make you a deal, how about if—"

"You've got nothing to bargain with. I don't need the notebook. I have the author sitting right over there. You had your chance." Jackson walked to the front of the stove. "Bring him over here. Bring that fat pig over here now!"

Michael jammed a rag into Jimmy's mouth and dragged him, kicking and screaming, to the stove. Rico grabbed hold of his neck and drove his head down, jamming his face into the burner. Jimmy could feel its sharp edges cutting into his skin.

"Have you ever smelled human flesh burning before, Dr. Paolucci?"

Edward didn't answer.

"I didn't think so. Actually, it's a fairly pleasant aroma. Sort of smells like chicken. And in this case, that's certainly appropriate. Wouldn't you say?" Jackson turned toward Michael. "Fire her up."

Jimmy was horrified. His bulging eyes followed Michael's hand as it crossed in front of his face and turned the black knob one notch to the right. The sound of the knob clicking into place sent a quiver through his bent body. A little red light above the knob lit and the burner began to warm.

"Normally, I prefer a gas range for cooking, but in this instance I think electric is much more effective. It takes a few minutes for the burner to respond, adding a bit of drama. The first few seconds are actually quite pleasant, almost like feeling the warmth of the sun on your face," Jackson said, leaning against the counter and calmly puffing on his cigar. "Unfortunately, it doesn't last long and it's all downhill from there I'm afraid. Your face is feeling nice and toasty right about now. Isn't it, Jimmy?" He leaned forward, looked him in the eye and smiled.

Jimmy fought to free himself but Rico and Michael held him tight. Unfortunately for him, one of his elbows found the side of Michael's face, just below the eye. Michael responded by grabbing a steak knife off the counter and slashing each of Jimmy's hamstrings, ending the struggle before it began. Robert and the others sat on the sofa and watched. Each wondered what would happen to them. They could hear the burner hiss as sweat rolled off Jimmy's face and dripped onto the hot surface.

"Crank it up all the way," Jackson ordered ruthlessly.

"Mmm…it's starting to smell like my old lady's cooking at a Friday night barbecue. The side of his face is gonna look like a bull's-eye," Johnny joked.

Jimmy's face trembled and his body quaked violently as the temperature jumped and the edge of the rings cut deeply into his skin. Searing pain shot through raw nerves and down his spine. The smell of his own flesh burning made him nauseous. Blood from his severed hamstrings rolled down the back of his legs and onto the floor. He prayed that he'd pass out, but never did. Jackson opened the refrigerator, poured himself a beer, and laughed.

*   *   *

Officers Joseph Picetti and Kevin O'Malley were less than an hour into their shift and on routine patrol when O'Malley noticed the red pickup parked on a side street adjacent to the Lafayette Hotel.

"Hey, Joe, swing by that pickup parked over there on Johnson Park. It fits the description of the one involved in the kidnaping at the fag bar a little while ago," Sergeant O'Malley said.

Officer Picetti flipped on the lights, swung the black and white around, and pulled up behind the truck. "Hey, you're right. The plate number matches the partial reported at the scene. I'll call it in and get some backup."

"I'm going in the hotel and see what I can dig up. The desk clerk is a two-bit punk I busted a few years ago on a B and E. I talked with the D.A.'s office and got his sentence reduced. Figured I'd need a favor some day," O'Malley said.

A second patrol car pulled up in front of the hotel five minutes later. Officers Thomas Graham and John Donovan were updated by Picetti as they entered the hotel.

"How's the family, Picetti?"

"Great, the twins are two and growing like weeds. They're agile, mobile, and hostile! I can't keep up with them, I don't know how Anne Marie does it all day long."

Officer Graham laughed. "I know where you're coming from. I've got four boys of my own."

The foyer was empty except for a bum passed out on the sofa, a regular by the name of Lenny Williams. An empty bottle of cheap whiskey, wrapped in a paper bag, rocked back and forth on the hardwood floor alongside the tattered sofa.

"They let anybody in here. Don't they?" O'Malley yelled as the three officers approached the front desk.

"Did you see old Lenny sacked out on the couch?" Graham asked.

"Yeah, he crashes here a few nights a week. I hear his old lady's cousin runs the dump," O'Malley replied. "We've got a possible hostage situation inside. There are three Caucasian males, at least one of which is armed and—"

"Save your breath, partner, I filled them in already," Picetti interrupted.

"Good deal. The clerk says they're in room two-oh-four. How about if Picetti and I take the stairs while you guys split up and cover both exits?" O'Malley asked.

"You got it. Let's go collar some bad guys," Donovan said.

Picetti stopped at the first landing, loaded six rounds into his shotgun and pumped the handle. "I've got a bad feeling about this. Something ain't right," he said.

*   *   *

"Let the fat bastard up," Jackson ordered.

Rico grabbed Callahan by the collar and jerked him from the burner. His burnt skin tugged at the hot coils before peeling away. Jimmy tried to stand but couldn't. He fell to the floor, curled up into a fetal position, and sobbed. The side of his face was bright red, almost orange and already beginning to blister. Small bits of flesh, still stuck to the burner, continued to smolder. The stench of burnt flesh permeated the room.

Rico lit a cigarette on the red-hot coils.

"Get that piece of crap to his feet and pull the rag out of his mouth," Jackson ordered.

Rico and Michael pulled Jimmy up and pinned him against the refrigerator.

Jackson picked up a salt shaker, unscrewed the top and poured a tablespoon into Jimmy's open wounds. "Where's the friggin' note-book?" he yelled.

Jimmy convulsed uncontrollably. The pain was unbearable. Rico squeezed his throat and slammed him into the refrigerator.

Callahan turned to Jackson and begged. "Please, no more. No more! I'll tell you everything. Don't hurt me anymore."

Jackson smiled. "Now that's the spirit of cooperation I've been look-ing for, Jimmy. Why did you have to make it so difficult on yourself?"

"Please, let me sit down. My legs hurt bad," Jimmy moaned.

"As soon as you tell me what I want to know. Tell me and I'll even give you something for the pain."

Jimmy lifted his arm and pointed to the ceiling just outside the bath-room. "There, it's up there, above the chipped tile," he said feebly. "Now, please, let me sit. I can't stand any longer. Please just let me sit down."

Jackson nodded. "Check it out, Rico. If you're lying to me, Jimmy, I'll jam your hand into the garbage disposal. I'll jam it in so far that you'll have to pick your nose with your elbow."

*　　　　　*　　　　　*

Charlie looked for an opening, any chance to escape. Johnny stood in front of them with a sawed-off shotgun draped across an arm and a pis-tol tucked in his pants. Michael was guarding Jimmy on the other side of the room, and Jackson was a couple of yards to his left. The pathway to the door was clear. All he needed was a small diversion. Perhaps when Rico opened the package in the ceiling. No one would be paying atten-tion to the three of them.

Rico holstered his gun and headed toward the bathroom. Charlie wasn't sure whether or not Jackson was carrying a weapon but he'd have to chance it anyway.

*   *   *

O'Malley and Picetti stood on either side of Jimmy's door and waited for Donovan to reach the alley. Officer Graham remained in the foyer.

*   *   *

Rico lifted the ceiling tile up and over. Jackson stood close by, anxiously looking on. Charlie noticed Jimmy crouching in his chair, slowly edging toward the floor.

"There's a couple of boxes up here all right. Hmm, that's weird, one's got a blinking red light. SHIT! It's wired, get—"

Charlie threw Robert and his father to the floor just as the charge ignited.

Shrapnel littered the air. Slivers of glass, metal and nails tore through everything. Rico never stood a chance. The left side of his body was cut to pieces, ribbons of flesh hung from his face. A long sliver of glass jutted from his eye. He fell from the chair, covered his face with his hands and begged for help. The strongbox fell from the ceiling, bounced off Rico's back before hitting the floor and rolling to a stop.

No one heard the gentle hissing of gas leaking from the ruptured line.

Jackson had managed to duck behind a chair a fraction of a second before the bomb went off, avoiding most of the shrapnel. Still, two nails and a four-inch piece of glass found their way into his right leg. He reached down and pulled the nails from his thigh but the piece of glass was buried too deep.

Shrapnel whizzed past Johnny's head as he dove to the floor behind the sofa, the same spot where Charlie, Robert and Edward were sprawled. Michael picked himself off the floor and rushed to help Rico.

The dust hadn't had a chance to settle before Jackson made his move. He crawled on his hands and knees, picked up the strongbox, got to his feet, and hobbled to the door. Rico flung himself at Jackson, latching onto a leg and begging for help.

"Get away from me," Jackson screamed, peeling Rico's hands from his leg and shoving him back to the floor.

"Police! No one move," O'Malley yelled, kicking in the door and quickly stepping inside the room. Officer Picetti was a step and a half behind. Jackson dropped to his knees, rolled to the side of the door and lay still.

*   *   *

Officer Graham heard the explosion from the foyer and called his partner on the walkie-talkie as he raced up the stairs two at a time.

"There's been an explosion on the second floor. I'm going up to check on O'Malley and Picetti. Evacuate the hotel and call for back up. Have them send fire and rescue units. I don't know what we're dealing with yet so go around front and fill everyone in when they arrive. I'll radio back when I get there. Do you copy?"

"Roger that, I'll call it in. The explosion's on the second floor all right. A couple of windows were blown out. Be careful, partner." Donovan clicked off his portable radio and sprinted toward the lobby. "Pull the fire alarm and clear the hotel!" he screamed as he rushed past the front desk clerk.

*   *   *

Michael drew his pistol and got off three rounds before Picetti dropped him with a single shotgun blast to the chest. His body flew backwards, crashing into the coffee table. Half of his upper back landed in a bloody mass on the sofa.

Michael's first two shots had missed their target but not the third. It caught O'Malley in the upper torso, collapsing a lung and shattering three ribs before lodging in his spine. His legs crumpled from under him and he tumbled to the floor.

Picetti was too busy rushing to his fallen partner's aid to notice Johnny rising to his feet. He was only two feet away when he heard the distinctive sound a shotgun makes when it's pumped.

Johnny stood less than ten feet away with a shotgun pointed at the police officer. "Kiss your fucking ass goodbye, cop," he snickered.

Charlie leaped across the room just as Johnny squeezed the trigger, but he was a split second too late. The force of the blast lifted Picetti off his feet. He crashed, upright, into the wall and slowly slid down it. A trail of blood followed his body to the floor. Officer Picetti's wife was a widow before her husband's body hit the ground. O'Malley lay paralyzed on the floor a few yards away.

Charlie fought with Johnny, trying desperately to gain control of the shotgun. They both fell to the floor, neither having an advantage.

The fire alarm sounded and in a matter of seconds the halls filled with scores of people fleeing their rooms.

Robert caught a glimpse of Jackson limping out the door with the strongbox tucked under an arm. He turned the corner and melted into the crowd of people, grinning as he ran past Officer Graham at the bottom of the stairs. Robert got to his feet, pulled his father up, and rushed to Charlie's aid.

"Forget about me. Go after Jackson," Charlie yelled.

Robert glanced at the door and back again at Charlie and hesitated.

"Do it!" Charlie shouted. "DO IT NOW! DAMN IT!"

Edward grabbed Robert's arm and pulled him away. "Come on. If Jackson gets away…everyone dies."

*   *   *

The foyer was chaos. Swarms of people squeezed down the staircase and funneled out through the exits. Donovan stood at the entrance futilely trying to restore order but was quickly deluged by the waves of people pouring out into the street. Jackson slithered his way through, over and around the crowd. Eventually making his way to the front door.

"There he goes!" Edward yelled.

"I see him! Let's get the bastard before he gets away," Robert said, fighting through the crowd as quickly as he could. He stepped on the porch a moment later. "Did you see which way he went?"

"Couldn't see from where I was. We'll have to split up. You go left down Johnson Park and I'll head up North Street toward Porter. Yell if you find him. Let's hope the bastard's still on foot."

Edward turned onto North Street a moment later and disappeared into the shadows.

God, it's dark out. It's like finding a needle in a haystack, Robert thought. He was half way down Johnson Park and about to turn back when he caught a glimpse of a shadow emerge from behind a garage and turn onto Tracy Street. "Got you! You, son-of-a-bitch," he whispered.

He ran through an alley, jumped over a rusted iron fence, and cut through a couple of backyards before coming up onto Tracy Street, a block and a half north of Jackson. He crouched down behind a stack of old tires on the side of an auto repair shop and waited.

*   *   *

Johnny hit Moore with a couple of solid blows to the face, sending him stumbling into the counter. He dove to the floor and grabbed hold of the shotgun before Charlie could recover.

"Well now, it looks like you shouldn't have sent your friends away. Seems you need their help after all," Johnny said, pumping the shotgun. "I'm really going to enjoy this."

"Hey, shit-for-brains! I'd take a nice long sniff before pulling the trigger if I were you."

Johnny swung around and found Jimmy sitting on the floor with his back propped up against the wall, holding O'Malley's service revolver in one hand and a cigarette lighter in the other.

"I'm sure even a neanderthal like you knows what natural gas smells like." Jimmy grimaced as pain shot through his body. "I'd say we're just about at critical mass. What do you think? Yep, I'd say there's enough gas in this room to send us all to hell and back. Go ahead, Johnny, pull the trigger. That should produce enough of a spark to set things off. Then again, maybe I should be the one to light us up." Jimmy said, raising the lighter over his head. "You're probably thinking I don't have big enough balls. Aren't you?"

"Take it easy Callahan. I'm putting the gun down, nice and slow. Don't do anything stupid. Okay?" Johnny placed the shotgun on the floor and took a few uneasy steps backwards. He glanced over his shoulder, checking the distance to the door.

"Don't even think about it, Johnny. Take a step towards the door and I light this place up. You'll be toast before you get three feet, dick-head!"

*   *   *

Robert leapt from the side of the building and tackled Jackson, driving him to the ground. Both men tumbled onto the front lawn. The strongbox rolled a few feet and came to rest on the edge of the sidewalk. Robert quickly recovered and grabbed Jackson by the back of the hair. He pounded the old man's face into the wet grass a few times before rolling him over and thrashing him with his bare hands.

Jackson never had a chance. He never saw him coming. He covered his face at first but Robert was too strong and too quick. After a short while, he wasn't able to lift a hand to defend himself. In the end, he just laid there and took a beating.

Robert grabbed the old man by the throat and squeezed, cutting off his air. Jackson's frail body quickly went limp as the last of his air was expended.

"What am I doing? I can't do this. Not even to scum like you," Robert said, releasing his grip and slowly rising to his feet. He could hear the sounds of Jackson gasping for air as picked up the box.

*   *   *

"Everything's cool now, Jimmy. I put the gun down. Let me go and I'll get you some help. I'll come right back. I promise, man. They'll fix you up real good. I'll make 'em, Jimmy. I didn't touch you. It was Rico and Michael. Not me! You know I was just following orders. It wasn't personal or nothing. Come on, Jimmy, you don't want to die. We've got to get out of here. Breathing this stuff ain't no good for you," Johnny pleaded.

"It's starting to smell like my old lady's cooking at a Friday night barbecue. Isn't that what you said, Johnny?" Callahan asked. "Get me a mirror," he ordered.

"You don't want a mirror. It looks pretty bad now but they can fix—"

"Shut up and get me a fucking mirror!"

Johnny pulled a mirror off the wall. Charlie stood still and watched. He could smell the gas fumes getting stronger.

Johnny lay the mirror on the floor and kicked it to Jimmy. He stepped back and pulled a switch blade from his back pocket.

Callahan placed the revolver on the floor and slowly lifted the mirror to his face. "Oh my God! Look what you've done to me! Jesus Christ! Look at my fucking face!" he cried.

"It wasn't me, Jimmy. It was Rico and—"

Jimmy smashed the mirror against the wall. "Fuck you. You son-of-a-bitch. I'll see you in hell!" He screamed, raising the lighter high into the air.

Johnny hurled the knife across the room, burying it deep into Jimmy's chest. His arm dropped sharply to his side, the lighter still clutched in his hand. Callahan grasped the pearl-handled knife, pulled it from his chest and dropped it on the floor. Blood trickled out at first but, within seconds, a stream flowed down his chest and collected in his lap. Johnny turned and sprinted for the door. Jimmy struggled to raise his arm again, lifting it a couple of feet off the ground. The corner of his lips curled into an eerie smile as his thumb pushed down on the small metal gear.

"Kiss your ass goodbye, motherfucker," he muttered.

Charlie leaped onto a chair and jumped through the window just as the gas ignited. The force of the explosion propelled his body a dozen feet from the side of the building. He landed on the hard concrete in the alley and was still conscious when he hit the ground. Fire and thick black smoke rolled out the windows above him. He could hear the sound of fire engines off in the distance. Johnny never made it to the door. His body lay on the floor, engulfed in a sea of fire and smoke.

*   *   *

Robert froze when he heard the sound of a gun being cocked behind him.

"You should have killed me when you had the chance, kid," Jackson said. His voice was hoarse and breath was shallow. "I won't make the same mistake. You can count on it."

Robert turned to find Jackson kneeling on one knee and holding a pistol in his hand.

He spit out a mouthful of blood. "You've been one colossal pain in the ass. Now put the box on the ground and step back," he ordered.

Jackson rose to his feet and walked toward him, holding the pistol firmly in his outstretched arm. He pushed the barrel of the gun up against Robert's forehead. "Looks like your luck's finally run out," he said grinning.

A single shot rang out and Robert's body jerked. A split-second later, Jackson's lifeless body lay on the wet grass. Edward stepped out of the shadows and tossed his gun on the ground at the dead man's feet.

✶   ✶   ✶

The Paoluccis arrived at the hotel just before Charlie was loaded into the ambulance.

He caught a glimpse of the metal box tucked under Robert's arm, smiled and turned his head. "I knew you'd get it back," he said. His breath was shallow and weak. "What about Jackson?"

"Dead," Robert answered.

"Good," Charlie said in a barely audible voice. "I need you to do something for me." He pulled Robert close and whispered in his ear.

"You sure?"

Charlie nodded and smiled faintly.

Robert reached into Charlie's jacket, pulled a flask from his pocket, and fed him a few sips.

"Ah! Now that's more like it. Thanks, doc."

"Thank you, Charlie. If it weren't for you—"

"Go on and get out of here. You've got a world to save. Don't worry about me. I've been in worse shape. I'll be back on my feet in no time."

Robert held his friend's hand and forced a smile. "I'll stop by and see you in the hospital."

Charlie Moore arrived at Buffalo General Hospital dead on arrival. He flat-lined in the ambulance at the same time that a patrol car discovered Daniel Jackson's body.

CHAPTER 24

Robert quickly stepped forward out of the reddish-orange glow. Edward stood still, opened his eyes slowly and looked around the room. His body was numb and tingling from head-to-toe.

"Don't worry, Dad, you get used to it," Robert said with a smile.

"It feels as though I have an electrical charge surging through by entire body," his father said, holding a hand in front of his face.

Robert slipped a CD into the laptop. "Actually, in a way. There is. The voltage is way too low to cause any problems though."

"How did we do?"

"We'll know in a few seconds, the CD's almost finished loading, just a little longer and…bingo! We're in business. Now let's see if everything's back the way it should be."

Edward leaned over his son's shoulder and watched. "Why do they call that thing a mouse anyway?"

Robert laughed. "I don't have a clue. I never really thought about it, to tell you the truth. Hey, here we are, the 1960 presidential election."

"Go to the next page," Edward prodded him.

Robert moved the pointer to the next page arrow, clicked the mouse button, and held his breath.

A split second later, a New York Times' headline filled the screen.

KENNEDY WINS CLOSE ELECTION

"Yes! We did it!" Robert yelled, jumping to his feet and hugging his father. "We did it."

"Son of a gun, it works! That thing really works! Doesn't it? I wouldn't have believed it if I hadn't seen it with my own eyes. None of what we've just been through has happened yet, has it?"

"No, none of it. We have a fresh start. Jimmy and Tony are still alive. Charlie's back at his office tossing Casey dinner scraps and Jackson's plane hasn't even landed in Buffalo yet. It's like starting all over again. Pretty weird, huh?"

"It's beyond weird. *Way* beyond weird!"

"Yeah, I guess you're right. It would make a great Twilight Zone episode though. Wouldn't it?"

"What's the Twilight Zone?"

Robert laughed. "It's a TV show that won't air for a few years yet. I grew up watching reruns on cable."

"What's cable?"

"Never mind," Robert said, shaking his head and laughing.

                *   *   *

Edward walked in from the balcony and stood next to his son. "It's time. You need to go back now."

"And what about you? I lose you all over again. Don't I?" Robert asked quietly.

Edward sat on the bed next to him. "I can take care of getting on the plane by myself. Whether I like it or not my time has come and there's nothing we can do to change that fact. We've both seen how dangerous change can be. It's my fate. Not yours, not JFK's, not even Molino and Callahan's. Your place is with your mother, there's nothing you can do for me here, not in this place and time. I'm already dead and you know it." He placed a hand on the back of Robert's neck and pulled him close, feeling the wetness of his son's tears against his face. "She needs you. I know you know that."

"But, what about me, I need both of—"

"Please let me finish," Edward interrupted. "I can't tell you how proud I am of you. I wish I could take the credit but your mom's the one that deserves it. You've given me a chance to see just what a fine man you've become and for that…I thank you. Before you go, I want you to know I love you more than anything in this world. Always have and always will." Edward stood, wiped away the tears, and walked to the window overlooking the garden.

"There's a quotation that I read a long time ago. I can't tell you who wrote it or exactly where I read it, but it's something that's stuck with me over the years. It goes something like this, '*What lies behind you and what lies before you are tiny matters when compared to what lies within you*'. I've seen what lies within you. From the time you were a skinny, freckle-faced seven-year-old boy catching frogs at Sinking Ponds to this man that stands before me today."

He turned away from the window and walked over to his son. "It's what lies in here that really matters," he said, holding his hand over Robert's heart. "It's the love in your heart and the character of your soul that matters most in life. You've grown up to be more of a man than I could have ever hoped for. I wish my Dad was here to see you too. But your destiny lies a thousand tomorrows from now, not here with me in this place and time. You need to let go of the past. Remember it, cherish it, and learn from it…but never live in it. You've got too much to live for and too much to give to let that happen." He smiled, leaned forward and kissed the top of his son's head. "I love you," he whispered. "Now let's hurry. I have a plane to catch."

               ★   ★   ★

"Don't worry about Callahan or Jackson. I'll make sure they never get their hands on my research. No one will, for that matter, and your equipment and photographs will go down with the plane. Are you ready?" Edward asked.

Robert flashed a thumbs up sign and smiled. "As ready as I'll ever be."

"Good. Give your mom a hug and kiss for me and tell her I love her with all my heart." Edward clicked on the mouse and stepped back.

Robert took a long last look at his father's face as the hard drive clicked and hummed.

"Oh! I almost forgot. Look under the white rock in the backyard when you get home. Okay?" Edward yelled.

"Did you say look under the white rock?" Robert asked as the light on the black box began to blink. He saw his father nod and a fraction of a second later, a pulsating red glow encased his body.

CHAPTER 25

1983

"And that's the last thing Dad said to me before I came back. That's why I dug up the rock. I know I must sound like I belong on Prozac or something but it's the truth. I'd never lie, not about Dad. You know that. Don't you?" Robert said, sitting alongside his mother, holding her hand.

His mother looked deeply into his eyes and offered a faint smile. "I believe you," she whispered as tears welled in her eyes. "Tell me about your father. Tell me how he looked, what he said, what he did. I want to hear everything."

Her son leaned forward and gently wiped the tears from her face. "He loved you very much. He asked me to tell you that. He didn't have to tell me though, I could see it in his eyes…in the way he looked at you."

*   *   *

"Dawn, it's Brian. I'm in the primate quarters and was wondering if you could stop by. There's something I want to show you."

"I'm pretty jammed up right now. What is it?" Dawn asked as she thumbed through her mail.

"Willie took a bad fall earlier this morning and was favoring his arm so I ran a bunch of X-rays and came across something weird. I don't have a clue to what it could be and wanted you to take a look."

"Stay put! I'm on my way."

Dawn arrived, half out of breath, at the primate quarters several minutes later. "What do you have?" she asked.

Brian Travis slipped an X-ray of Willie's forearm up under the clip and turned on the light. "He's got a slight fracture of the radius, on the posterior side, about three and a half inches below his elbow," he said running his finger on the X-ray, along the fracture line.

Dawn stepped forward and examined the break. "Yep, that's a fracture all right. We'll have to put a soft cast on him for a couple of weeks. But what's so unusual about that? It looks like your run-of-the-mill fracture to me."

"Take a look at this," Brian said, slipping another X-ray alongside the first. "This is a film of the same arm only from the anterior side."

"What the hell is that?" Dawn asked, taking another step forward.

"Don't know. I've never seen anything like it."

Dawn picked up a magnifying glass and held it close to the X-ray. "It's manmade. That's for sure. Its edges are too uniform to be natural. Looks about the same size as a dime, only a little thicker. It's definitely metal. It's not buried too deep. Looks to be just below the epidermis." She put the magnifying glass down and turned toward Brian. "Where's Willie?"

"I had to put him under to run the X-rays. He's still out cold in the recovery room."

"How much longer do you suppose he'll be out?"

"At least another hour."

"Good, grab a surgical kit and meet me there. I'm going to take it out."

Dawn finished shaving Willie's forearm a few minutes later. She studied the X-ray, made a small transverse incision just below his elbow, retracted his skin, and began to probe. Less than a minute passed before she located and removed the biochip from the chimp's arm.

"What is it?" Brian asked, peering over her shoulder.

Dawn washed the chip in a saline solution and held it up to the light. "I don't know. I've never seen anything like it," she replied. "It's some sort of a miniature electronic device."

"How long you suppose it's been in there?"

"Look at the calcification on its surface. I'd say it's been in there for a long time. At least twenty years, maybe longer."

"It couldn't have been. They didn't have this technology in the early sixties. Christ, I don't even think the transistor was invented back then."

Dawn stepped back from the operating table and slid her mask down. "It wasn't," she said, taking her latex gloves off and tossing them into the garbage. "Would you sew Willie up and put a soft cast on him? I'm going to bring this back to my office for a closer look."

"Not a problem."

"Oh, and do me another favor, will you?"

"What's that?"

"Keep this to yourself for now. Don't tell anyone until I speak with you again."

Brian hesitated for a moment before nodding. "Who do you think put that in his arm?"

"That's what I'm going to try and find out." She slipped the chip into a petri dish and hurried back to her office. *I'll bet my house that Robert Paolucci has something to do with this,* she thought.

Dawn sat at her desk, flipped through the Rolodex and picked up the phone. "I'm dying to find out what he'll have to say," she muttered to herself.

Suddenly, her office door slammed closed and a man, with a gun, stepped out from behind the door.

"Please put the phone down, Dr. Mackey. Do as I ask and I won't harm you. You have my word," he said quietly.

"Who are you? And what do you want?" she asked nervously.

"My name's Jimmy Callahan and don't worry, I don't want anything from you. No, ma'am, all I'm after are a few minutes of your boyfriend's time." Jimmy locked the door, walked to the window and drew the shades closed.

"There must be some mistake, I don't have a boyfriend. I'm not seeing anyone."

"Well, I don't know what you want to call him but I saw you at his house a few days back and the two of you at the Parkside Bar the day before yesterday."

"Are you talking about Robert Paolucci?"

"Bingo! Give the lady a cigar."

"He's not my boyfriend! I only met him a few days ago."

"Whatever! I don't a rat's ass what he is to you. All I know is that he'll be here if he thinks you're in trouble."

"What is it you want?"

"You'll find out soon enough. I need to borrow your phone for a minute, if you don't mind. Don't worry, it's a local call," Jimmy snickered.

*   *   *

Helen opened the envelope and began to read the letter her husband had left for her just as the phone rang. "I'll get it. Why don't you get yourself cleaned up. You look awful," she said.

Robert nodded and headed to the bathroom as his mother walked to the kitchen to answer the phone. He had just turned on the water when he heard his mother calling his name.

"Pick up the phone. It's for you," she yelled.

"Take a message, will you? I'll call back later." He put his hands under the faucet and drew the water up to his face. The warm water felt comforting, almost therapeutic.

"He says it's important. He needs to talk with you right away."

"Who is it?"

A moment went by before she responded. "It's Jimmy."

He raced out of the bathroom and grabbed the phone. "Who the hell is this?"

"It's, Jimmy…Jimmy Callahan. Remember me?"

Robert's stomach sank and his heart raced. "No friggin' way. There's no way it's you."

"Believe me it is. I did a little time traveling myself, doc."

"How?" Robert asked. A thousand thoughts raced through his head.

"I'll explain that when I see you. You've got thirty minutes to meet with me. Not a minute more."

"And if I don't? What are you going to do?"

"I'll kill the veterinarian girlfriend of yours. It would be a shame to kill her, she's such a pretty little thing…and smart too!"

"Dawn Mackey?"

Jimmy wet his lips with his tongue and smiled. "Yep, that's the one. She's here, sitting next to me."

"What do you want, you fat piece-of-shit?"

"Tick-tock. Tick-tock. The clock's running, doc. Meet me at her office and bring your equipment. You've got a little more than twenty-nine minutes and don't be stupid. Don't call the police. I've got every-thing bugged. You fuck with me and I'll feed the bitch to the lions. Right after I let the gorillas bang the shit out of her."

*   *   *

Robert's footsteps echoed in the corridor as he slowly approached Dawn's office. The hallway was dark except for the thin slice of light escaping from under her door. He swung his backpack down off his shoulder, held it in one hand, and knocked.

The door swung open and Callahan stepped into the doorway, clutching a pistol in his hand. His chubby face sported an arrogant grin. "Howdy, doc! I told you he'd come, Dr. Mackey. Right on time as usual," he said, glancing at his watch. He turned toward Robert and held out his hand. "What's it been? Twenty years? Why you don't look as though you've aged a bit, Dr. Finaldi. Or should I say, Dr. Paolucci?"

"Are you all right, Dawn?" Robert asked, pushing away Jimmy's hand and stepping towards her.

Dawn nodded. "What's going on?" she asked.

Robert turned back toward Jimmy and looked him in the eye. "You got what you wanted. I'm here. Now let her go. She's got nothing to do with this. It's between you and me."

"In due time professor. All in due time. You have my word on it."

"Your word's good for shit!"

"Maybe it is, but then again, what choice do you have? My request is quite simple. All I want is to go home. I'd do it myself but I loaned my ruby red slippers to Dorothy. If you catch my drift."

"So that's it. All I have to do is send you back and you'll let her go?"

"Yep."

"Why do you need him to go back home? Why don't you just take a plane yourself?" Dawn asked.

"It's a wee bit more complicated than that, sweetheart," Callahan said. "Home's a couple of decades ago. The eighties are interesting but I'm an old-fashioned kind of a guy. I need the good doctor's help to return to a time when Elvis was thin and JFK was still a senator from Massachusetts. I need your boyfriend's time machine."

Dawn sat back in her chair, pushed the hair from her face and turned toward Robert. "You're the one who left Willie in the park. You sent him back in time. Didn't you?" She held up the biochip. "You're the one who put this in his arm. You're not doing research on chimps. You just wanted to see him. You wanted to see how he held up. It all makes sense now. That's why he reacted the way he did to you at the zoo the other day. He's your chimp."

Robert nodded. "I'm sorry I lied to you but I couldn't exactly tell you the truth. I didn't expect anything would come of it. I certainly didn't expect this."

"Enough chitchat. You two lovebirds can catch up later. Now, doc, if you'd be so kind as to set your equipment up."

Robert put his backpack on Dawn's desk and unloaded the laptop and black box. "How exactly did you manage to get back here?"

"I was in your hotel room, hiding in the closet when your dip-shit father sent you back to the future. He left the room for a while and I used the equipment to travel back here. It was a piece of cake."

"What photograph did you use?"

"One of the ones you gave to him before you left. It was touching that you wanted him to have a picture of you but not exactly a smart thing to do, huh? I've been back here for a little less than a week now and have been tailing you ever since. I was even at the Parkside Bar when the two of you had lunch."

Robert connected a cable to the serial port and ran it to the black box. He plugged the computer in and hit the start button. "Why go back? Why not stay here?" he asked.

"Christ, I thought the sixties were fucked up until I came here. You can't even get laid without worrying about AIDS. Besides, I'll have a lot more financial opportunities back there."

"How's that?" Robert asked.

"I just happen to know which companies will do well, and who will win the World Series and Super Bowls for the next twenty-three years. I'll parlay that knowledge into a ton of cash and the best thing about it is that it'll be legit. The feds won't be able to touch me. Yep, I'll be living high off the hog!"

"It's all about money. Isn't it?"

Jimmy smiled and nodded. "Damn right it is."

"So how do you know I won't travel back and stop you?"

Callahan grinned. "I spent some time at UB and came across the nicest bunch of computer hackers a guy could meet. They were kind enough to give me a virus that totally wipes out the hard drive." He pulled a floppy disk from his pocket. "If you'll allow me, professor." He loaded the disk and transferred a file to the hard drive. "There we go. The hard drive will crash in five minutes and all your files will be permanently trashed. So you can't follow me back, doc. No one can. Here, slip this picture into the black box and let me know when your ready."

Robert snatched the picture, fit it into the holder, and hit the close button. "It's ready."

"Good, now get your ass to the corner."

Jimmy walked over to the computer, hit several keys and waited for the program to load. "I can't take a chance that you don't have another one of these gadgets laying around somewhere and will follow me back, now can I, doc?" He raised the gun from his side and squeezed the trigger three times.

Robert never had a chance. The force of the bullets sent him crashing to the floor and blood quickly soaked through his shirt. Dawn screamed and rushed toward him. She draped herself over his motionless body, trying desperately to stop the bleeding. "You've killed him you son-of-a-bitch!"

Jimmy stepped forward, raised the gun again and pointed it at her head. Dawn closed her eyes and turned away.

"Sorry, ma'am, but I lied. I can't leave any loose ends. It's nothing personal. Just business," he said, pulling the trigger.

The gun jammed. Jimmy squeezed the trigger a half dozen times and still nothing happened. Dawn's heart skipped a beat and her body trembled each time the chamber rotated and the hammer clicked.

"Shit, the damn thing's broken." The hard drive hummed and the red light blinked. "Crap, I'm out of time. This must be your lucky day," he said as he stepped in front of the black box.

Dawn opened her eyes just in time to see his large silhouette fade into the reddish-orange light and disappear a split-second later. After a few more seconds, the hard drive on the computer crashed and the screen went blank. She sat on the floor in front of Robert, unable to move or speak. Her body trembled uncontrollably. She leaned forward, pulled her knees tight to her chest, buried her head in her hands, and cried.

"Hey, can you give me a hand here?"

Dawn spun sharply and found Robert struggling to sit up.

"Oh my God! I thought you were dead."

He grabbed hold of his shirt and popped the buttons. "Nope, I came prepared. I borrowed a bullet proof vest from by cousin. He's a cop at the fourteenth precinct. See," he said, holding his shirt open wide, exposing the vest with three 44 caliber bullets wedged in the upper chest.

"What about all the blood?"

"I swung by my lab on the way over here and picked up a few pints of blood. I taped 'em to the front of the vest just to make it look real."

"Well, you sure fooled me."

"Sorry, but I didn't exactly have a chance to tell you."

"Jimmy got away. He went back," Dawn said.

Robert shook his head. "No he didn't. I modified the computer program before I got here. He didn't travel anywhere. His molecules were digitalized and stored in a file on the hard drive. The irony is that he did himself in by crashing the computer. He destroyed all the files...including his."

"You mean he's dead?"

"Yep, done in by a virus. A computer virus, nonetheless."

Dawn helped him to his feet. "How are you feeling?"

He put his hand on the back of his head and grimaced. "My head's killing me. I hit it on the floor when I fell and everything went blank. I can't believe how much those bullets hurt. I bet I'm going to have some nasty looking welts," he said.

"You were out cold for half a minute or so."

"Can I ask you a personal question?" Robert asked with a mischievous grin.

"Sure, go ahead."

"Did you try and revive me by giving me mouth-to-mouth resuscitation?"

Dawn smiled. "I didn't have time. Jimmy had a gun pointed at my head. You still look a little woozy to me though. Do you suppose it'll help if I try it now?"

He put his arms around her and pulled her close. "Most definitely."

She leaned forward and gently kissed his lips. "How's that?"

"I'm feeling a *little* better but I think it's going to be a slow recovery. One which will require *quite* a bit more first-aid."

"I see. Well we better get started then. Shouldn't we?"

"Whatever you say. You're the doctor!"

9 780595 203109